WITHIN THE

SHADOWS

J.A. Lynch

Design by:
Vivid Book Design
Cover picture from Stock

Vamptasy Publishing
An Imprint of Crushing Hearts and Black Butterfly
Publishing

For my nephew, Liam,
the brightest star in the sky.

A huge thank you to: my parents, Maurice and Patsy, for their continued love and support, for picking me up whenever life got me down and putting faith in me and my dreams; my little sisters, Genevieve and Pamela, who have helped and encouraged me over the years, thank you for listening to me whittle on for hours about my dreams and for reading draft after draft, I value your support, even though you both drive me mad; my husband, Sean, you have been there for me for the best part of my life and have inspired me in more ways, I doubt you'll ever know the true value of my love for you; my five children, Kristopher, Kelly, Matthew, Rory & Poppy, you are my greatest achievement yet, and I hope I inspire you to take on your own dreams; Amy for listening to me, showing me valued support and giving me great advice when I needed it; and last but not least, Nicola, for taking a gamble, and helping turn my dreams into a reality, you will never know how grateful I am.

"Part of every misery is, so to speak, the misery's shadow or reflection: the fact that you don't merely suffer but have to keep on thinking about the fact that you suffer. I not only live each endless day in grief, but live each day thinking about living each day in grief."

C.S. Lewis

Waking up is considered a simple daily task to most, but for me, lying so still and lifeless scares me. The haunting echo of confusion filled my head with pain and a hunger for something I do not know. The burning that spreads throughout my body is something I cannot describe without wanting to wail and escape the anguish that keeps building up.

Here I am, in a situation that can only be described as a nightmare. For me, this is no dream. Today I was reborn into a world full of darkness and horror. My place is unknown to me, but the desire to feed is my basic instinct.

My name is Giselle Bergman. I'm eighteen-years-old and from what I can remember I have lived a good, yet short life.

Within the Shadows

Chapter 1

I felt his eyes on me before I returned the look. He knew what I was thinking and, like always, he knew the right way to cheer me up. Best friends were like that and Alex was, without a doubt, my knight in shining armour. He was like my shadow and the last six years proved to me just how dependable he had become.

"We need sugar and lots of it," he practically shouted, pulling into the lot.

"But we'll be late for school! I can *not* have another detention, Alex, and besides, I need to see Marc before class," I sighed.

"Well, Marc can wait. Strawberry glaze or chocolate sprinkles?" he asked me as he got out of the car.

Alex winked at me, and I giggled like a little girl following him.

"One of each," I said. "It's a Monday. I need me some sugar."

Grabbing hold of his arm, I held onto him and ignored the sneering looks from a group of girls leaving the cafe.

"Still slumming it, I see, Alex. Call me when you man up," the local slut hollered as she walked across the lot with her minions in tow.

I ignored them and their taunts and walked inside, escaping to our favourite table. "Bitches," I scowled, looking out the window. "Who does she think she is?" My face reddened with anger.

"Ignore her, G. She's harmless."

"Why are you always defending her?" My voice was now an octave above a whisper.

Grabbing the menu from me, he threw it onto the table. "Look at me . . . They can say whatever they want. They can make as many comments and it won't change a thing. You're my friend, Giselle. And besides, you look *way* better than them."

Laughing, I looked back outside and watched Evie with her perfect body driving off in her perfect car as I felt sick inside.

"Marc seems to think she's great." My voice croaked as I watched her drive off.

"Marc's an ass," Alex said as he looked over the menu, pouting his lips at whatever he fancied. He did that when something appealed to him.

"Alex!"

"Well, think about it. He's dating you and yet he has time for said 'bitches.' Give me a break. If you were my girlfriend, and this is just hypothetical, I wouldn't let you out of sight or give those asses reason to pick on you, but that's just from my viewpoint. Now, let's order. I am starving."

The small bistro was buzzing with customers. The delicious scent of freshly made coffee filled the air; it woke up my taste buds. Its bright and bold colours hurt my eyes. Shades of orange, lime green, and sunbeam yellow had been painted abstractly on the walls, reminding me of summer. Even the ceiling reminded me of the ocean with its cool shades of baby blue. Somehow, it had become a place of comfort to me. The people reminded me that I belonged here and, like always, Marion was the first to come welcome us and take our order.

"Morning, you two. The usual?" she asked. Turning to face me, she smiled and her voice softened. "How is your mother, Giselle?"

"Hi, Marion, um, yeah, the usual, but can I have a side order of arsenic to go?" I laughed. "Um, Mom is good, thanks."

"That's great, sweetheart. Give her my love." Laughing, she walked back towards the counter, shaking her head.

Alex sat forward, his brilliant green eyes staring hard into mine. "Arsenic?"

"Well, it was either that or crushed glass."

We both burst out laughing, getting the attention of the people on the table next to us. We were like two naughty school children. Giggling as we ate, we didn't care who scowled at us. It was just Alex and I, in our own world and nothing was going to break that bond . . . ever.

Of course, the ride to school was becoming increasingly uncomfortable. My pain increased with each kilometre the closer we got to school. I knew I had to face Marc at some point in the day, but to be honest, I was too pissed off with him to really care about why he had dropped me for some lame party in town.

My stomach spun and I was nervous as I got out of the car. Marc was standing over by his truck on the far side of the lot and there was no avoiding him. He stood with Aaron and Doug, his best friends, and watched me as I tried my best not to look at him. But it was so hard. He and his beautiful puppy dog eyes always got to me and I knew I would be putty in his hands.

Yet, I wanted him to squirm just a little while longer, for my own benefit. Alex swung his arm over my shoulder and pulled me in close to him, reassuring me that my impending confrontation would be fine. I wished I had his confidence in me.

"Relax. Just keep eye contact and scowl. Scowl like a mad woman," he whispered as we parted company. "Laters, Bergman." And he was gone.

I was on my own.

Marc eyeballed me as I slowly made my way over to him. The bell rang and people bumped past me as they rushed off to homeroom. I, on the other hand, had to lay a few things to rest before I could face my day of boredom and its side helping of bitchiness.

"Hi!" I greeted all three of them.

"Um, morning, G," Aaron said as he nudged Doug in the arm.

Guys must have some sort of secret code, because without Aaron saying anything, they both looked at each other, then at Marc, and left.

"You took your time coming in today," Marc said as he slung his bag over his shoulder.

"Yeah, but that's my business," I bitterly retorted.

"G, you're meant to be my girlfriend. Maybe you should start acting like it."

"What? Are you for real? You're such an ass, Marc." Anger began to boil inside me and I walked on ahead of him.

"Giselle, wait," he called after me. "I'm sorry."

"Sorry doesn't even cut it, Marc," I sighed. "You blew me off for what? Drinks with the 'guys.' I went to so much trouble. Can you imagine how dumb I felt waiting for you to turn up?"

"I really am sorry. I didn't know that Andy was going to some frat house. If I had known, I wouldn't have gotten into the car. I swear, G, I would have shown up. Only, things got out of hand." His eyes shot to the ground, avoiding having to look at me.

It was so hard staying mad at him. I really wanted him to grovel more and feel like total shit, but I couldn't do it to him. I adored him and wanted to make up so badly.

7

"It was our anniversary, Marc. Four years is a pretty big deal, but, you can make it up to me," I said coyly.

Looking up into his delicious blue eyes, I felt my anger melt and I was more than ready for our make-up kiss. Pulling me in close to him, he cupped my face in his hands and gently pulled my mouth to his. I could smell his cologne, and as it danced in circles around my nostrils, I kissed him back, our tongues lightly brushing together. The kiss got a few whistles of approval and a stern mouthful from Mr. Green.

"What is the meaning of this public display of . . . of . . ." he stuttered.

"Affection," Marc tried to finish the line for him.

I held in my laughter as he led us into the school and straight to Principal Brooks' office. Standing outside of Brooks' office, neither Marc, nor I, said anything, but his smile said it all. We were back on track.

"Bergman, Clark, g . . . g . . . get in here now," Green bellowed from the doorway.

Marc entered the office first and I hastily stopped at the door, avoiding eye contact with Brooks.

"Bergman, close the door when you've decided to join us," Green said sarcastically as he folded his arms. His face was red and swollen, and by the looks of things, the night before had been a heavy one. Everyone knew he was a little too fond of the booze.

"Giselle, come in and close the door," Principal Brooks directed me.

Obediently, I shut the door behind me and stood close to Marc, trying my best not to laugh. When I get nervous, I tend to mask my feelings by laughing or making light of the situation, but right then and there, I doubted my humour would have been appreciated.

"Giselle, I am very disappointed in you. How many times have we had this discussion? You are always late for school, you're behind in your assignments, and, to be blunt, I am getting quite sick of your casual display of affection with Mr. Clark."

I could not believe it. He was pinning it all on me! "But . . ." I tried to speak.

"Enough of your excuses! You're on detention for the rest of the week. I believe you should be in English, and if you make it quick, I am sure Ms. Royston won't add to your ever-growing record of disobedience." He ushered me out of the room. "Marc, this game on Friday night . . ." The door closed and the conversation became nothing more than muffled voices.

As I made my way to class, I could not have felt more pissed off. Walking into the already quiet classroom was bad enough, but having Evie smugly looking at me as I fumbled through my bag was the last straw.

"When you're ready, Giselle," Ms.Royston said.

Sitting down, I looked around for Alex, and there he sat, smiling at me, showing concern with those luminous green eyes, and instantly I felt calm.

"You okay?" he mouthed at me.

Nodding my head, I tried not to distract Ms. Royston, but failed.

"Is there something you'd like to share with the rest of the class, Giselle?" she asked me.

I could feel my cheeks going red and my heart pounded hard in my chest. "No." My voice quivered.

Everyone was looking at me and I could feel Evie's eyes staring hard at me, but I refused to give in and just stared ahead.

"Really? Well, maybe you can take part in our class discussion. What is Atticus's relationship to his children like?" She sat back against her desk and folded her arms, waiting for my input.

Oh my God, I thought. I had read the book, well, only slightly, but God, I didn't have a clue. My face became redder and redder as I slowly died inside.

Alex spoke up. "Atticus is a kind, and I suppose, loving father. He reads to his children and offers them comfort when they need it. He is also capable of teaching them pretty harsh lessons, like when he allows Jem to come with him to tell Helen Robinson about Tom's death, but he is also a very wise man, one who is committed to justice and equality, and his parenting style is based on fostering these virtues in his children. He even encourages Jem and Scout to call him "Atticus" so that they can interact on terms as equal as possible. Well, that is what Giselle and I discussed earlier." He confidently sat back in his chair and grinned at me.

"Well, that was . . ." Ms.Royston began, but then the bell rang and I was out of that room in a flash.

I stood by my locker, defeated by Monday's usual round up, and I craved my warm bed. I wanted to escape the usual bullshit of school life and wanted nothing more than to run away, to live my life far from there on the other side of the world.

"It can't be that bad," Alex said as he stood beside me.

"Wanna bet? I have just had the worst morning ever. I was hauled in by Green for kissing Marc and now Brooks has me on another week of detention. My dad is gonna kill me." Closing my eyes, I inhaled a deep breath.

"Ouch! But at least you have the prom on Saturday. That is something to look forward to, right?" He tried his best to make me feel better.

"With the way my week's going, I doubt I'll make it to Saturday."

"Oh, come on, G, play it cool. Just keep your head down and for God's sake, stay out of Green's way," he said as he hugged me.

"Yep, but that's easier said than done."

The noise from the corridor began to fade and the bell rang again. I had an awful knack for being late for everything, and at this rate, I was more than likely going to be late for my own funeral.

"See you later. I gotta go dazzle the lovely Ms. Shultze." He winked at me and left me alone.

I stood with my eyes closed for a few moments, trying my hardest not to succumb to the overwhelming feelings growing inside me. I wanted to cry. Hell, I wanted to throw a tantrum that a two-year-old could get away with, but knowing the endless chaos it would bring would probably ruin my school life forever. I played it safe and held my emotions in, like always.

Opening my locker, I searched for my algebra book. "Damned thing," I cursed to myself. –Instead I found a sealed brown envelope, lodged between my music folder and my copy of *To Kill A Mockingbird*.

Pulling it out, I looked it over, then checked the corridor for any peering eyes and opened the blank envelope. Inside, I found a disc and a small note. There was nothing else. That was when I decided to let my curiosity get the best of me. The message had been pieced together with cut-outs from magazines, but it was the words that had the profoundest effect on me.

Once upon a time, a girl had a dream. She had the boy. She had it all. Now it's time to burst that bubble.

Without hesitating, I skipped the rest of the day's lessons. I knew no one would be home when I got there. Dad was away on another business trip and Mom was more than likely planning some charity convention with the other contenders for 'Mother of the Year.'

Grabbing a bag of chips and a can of Pepsi from the refrigerator, I casually strolled into the family room, sliding the disc into the DVD player and pressing play. Sitting back on the sofa, I chugged down half the can and started munching on my favourite snacks. Before I could swallow my mouthful, what I saw caught me completely off guard. Struggling to control the ever-growing knot in my stomach, my eyes filled with tears. I was torn in two, full of disbelief at what I was seeing and anger that this was no set up. I wanted to scream, but my voice would not come out.

Breathe, Giselle. Breathe.

That was when reality really hit me and I started screaming with uncontrollable sobs and tears that fell down my cheeks. My head pulsated as I searched through my bag for my phone whilst the audio played in the background. *Her* laughter and moans filled my head, and in a rage I threw the controller at the TV screen. It cracked and the screen went dead momentarily.

Frantically, I dialled Alex's number and paced, waiting for him to answer.

"Hello?" he answered.

"Alex . . . Alex . . ." I sobbed.

"Giselle, what's wrong?" he asked, concerned.

"Oh God . . . Marc and . . . he . . ." I broke down.

"Where are you?" he asked.

"Home."

Sitting on the floor in the middle of the room, I cried. Inside, my stomach churned over and over, and at times, I felt like vomiting, but it didn't happen. Instead, I inhaled long deep breaths to counteract my sobs. Dizziness plagued me as I tried to make sense of what I had just seen. Surely, it had been some kind of sick joke, but it was too real. Marc had to have known about this, but I was at a loss as to what to do. If it was true, then things would never be the same again, and inside, I could feel a part of me die.

Chapter 2

Alex sat beside me on the lounge floor and held the empty envelope in his hands. His face was no longer that of the calm handsome guy I had known for so long. Instead, his jaw was clenched tight and his eyes were wild.

Looking around the room, he let out a long breath and then stood up. Walking over to the television, he lifted the controller from the floor and pressed play. He stood back from the screen and watched the footage through the cracks.

"I am going to kill that son of a bitch," he seethed.

Hearing the audio a second time round made it all the more real. I avoided staring at the screen, and the more I listened, the more I realised I had to do something about it.

"My dad is going to kill me," I blurted out.

"What!" Alex exclaimed.

Walking over to the television, I pulled the power cord out of the wall and stood back from the screen. "I broke it."

"Yeah, but, I'll sort that out. Giselle, what are we going to do about Marc?" he asked.

I just looked at him, surprised that he was so worked up over this and curious as to what he had in mind. "Confront him, I guess."

"Oh, no. We're going to do more than confront him," he shouted.

Up until now, I had never really seen Alex lose his composure, but here he was almost ready to burst and it was all over something Marc had done to me, not him.

"I . . . don't know what to do." I broke down and he held me.

Holding me close and refusing to break the embrace, Alex gently stroked my hair as I tried hard to compose myself while failing at every breath.

"We will humiliate him in front of the whole school, both of them," he said.

"What?"

"At prom . . . There would be no better revenge. Think about it, G. The ultimate payback."

I pulled away from him and walked over to my mother's favourite day chair and sat down. Running my hands through my hair, I looked out of the large bay window and watched the branches of the large willow tree sway from side to side.

"I am not sure. What do you suggest?"

Laughing, he came over and sat on the ground by my legs. "Think, big television, playback, and an audience that would love the entertainment. Obviously, you would have to try your best over the next five days or so, you know, to pretend that everything is fine, but I can assure you, it would be the ultimate revenge, and I swear there would be no comeback on you."

"Alex, this is crazy. I can't . . . I am not that strong."

"G, you are stronger than you think, and I will be with you every step of the way. I will not let you down like that loser. I am not like him."

"I don't know. This is all too much," I shouted.

Taking my hands into his, he lowered his voice. "Do you trust me?"

"Of course, I trust you, Alex, but not even you can fix this," I said, defeated.

"I can assure you I can do a lot. Leave it all to me. Just make sure you show up that night and the rest will reveal itself," he said earnestly.

The clock on the mantel piece chimed and both of us got to our feet. A car door shut and footsteps made their way towards the front door. It was my mother and the room was a mess. Alex ran over to the television and lifted out the game controllers. He threw one at me and promptly slipped a disc into the PlayStation. The door opened and in walked my mother.

"Giselle, what are you doing home so early?" she asked as she slipped off her shoes and walked toward the room.

"I, um, felt unwell and took the rest of the day off."

Walking into the room, she caught sight of Alex and then the television. "What on earth has happened here?" she shouted as she examined the crack across the television.

"Hi, Mrs. Bergman. I came round to cheer Giselle up and we got carried away with the game. It was my fault and I have already contacted my father who is more than willing to pay for the damage." His voice was calm and confident.

"There is no need for that, Alex. I am sure your father has better things to do than spend his money on minor incidents," she said, smiling at Alex.

"My father won't hear of it, and I do feel responsible, so please accept it. God knows when he'll cough up money again!" Alex laughed.

My mother was all doe-eyed, and for a moment, it looked as though she had been put under a spell. Fortunately, she came round pretty quickly and gave me a sharp look. She turned her back on us and walked out of the room. She had been looking so pale as of late, yet her robust personality was enough to make you stand to attention when she came into a room. That is not to say that my mother was not pleasant as she had a way of making people adore her. With prom coming up, she was in her glory.

"Told you I'd sort it out. Trust me, Giselle. Okay?" Alex said, breaking the silence.

"Okay," I answered and sat back down on the chair, giving in to my feelings.

***

The week passed by in what seemed like a blur. I went through all the motions of being the dutiful girlfriend. I laughed at all the right jokes and even stomached displays of affection. Underneath it all, I was dying, or at least it felt like I was dying.

Prom night finally came.

Looking in the mirror, I could hardly recognize myself. I knew it was me, but what I felt on the inside did not show on the outside. The dark blue elegant dress was dramatic and complemented my complexion. The gorgeous peau de soie satin gown was detailed at the bust line with dazzling crystal stones. Tiny little beaded flowers sat across the bodice and glimmered when the light shone on them. The lace-up back was stunning with ties adorned with crystals. I looked every inch of perfection.

My phone rang and distracted me from my moment of pure horror. "Hello!" I said.

"You ready for payback, princess?" Alex asked in his usual carefree manner.

Sighing, I could barely talk and whispered a weak, "I guess."

"I'll see you there. All is set. I just need the duo in the same room. Catch you later, Bergman."

Before I could say 'bye,' he had hung up on me and I was alone again with some serious thoughts of self-destruction. Of course, the calls from my mother soon put a stop to that.

"Giselle, Giselle, honey. Marc is here," she bellowed from the bottom of the stairs.

"Two seconds, Mom," I yelled back.

19

Breathe, just breathe through it, I thought to myself as I walked down the stairs toward the waiting chaos.

I swear I could see tears in my mother's eyes and my dad stood looking at me proudly. My brothers were taking the proverbial piss out of me, which was the usual, but it was Marc who I avoided looking at. He made me sick.

Marc and I stood together in front of the camera, smiling as if we had just won the lottery, but underneath the façade I was aching inside. I was tormenting myself, going over every little detail, and blaming myself. After all, he was just a guy and had to get '*it*' from somewhere, and as Greg had so cordially said in the past, I '*wasn't putting out.*'

I felt so betrayed and annoyed that he willingly threw four years of dating away just to lose his virginity to a skank, and not just any skank, either. It was Evie Stokes, of all people. I could feel the anger swelling up inside my stomach. I thought I would throw up right there in front of my parents.

"Oh my gosh, aren't they just adorable?" my mother gushed, squeezing my father's hand.

Sometimes, she made me sick, and right now, I felt pretty angry with her for making me go through with it all. My mother was the type of woman who would tread on people to get to the front of the queue. Hell, my mother was more than that. She was the queen bee and boy, did we know it, but she was also my best friend and I could not refuse her this moment.

I did not intend standing there for much longer as Marc's hand rested casually upon my waist. "Okay, enough of the pictures. We have a prom to get to," I seethed as I hurried to the door.

I stared at Marc's emotionless face. God, he was gorgeous. I could not deny him that. I only wished he had waited for me and had the patience to do so until I was ready. But in typical guy style, he blew it.

"Oh, sweetie, just one more," my ever irritating mother yelped, grabbing the camera from my father.

Snap. One more for the album.

Marc followed me on cue out the door and into the chill of the night. "So what's the deal, Giselle? Why the cold shoulder?" he asked, convincingly angelic.

I did not answer. I got into the back of the limo and waited for him. I wished that what I had seen were not true. I loved him so much. I was convinced we would be going to college together as we had planned. Things just would not be the same without him, but it was something I would have to get used to.

It broke my heart.

***

The ride to *Le Meridien Hotel* was short. Closing my eyes, I inhaled deeply, readying myself for the night ahead. I had thought about caving in and forgetting about my plans, but something inside spurred me on. I had to do this, for me.

Inside, the theme sickened me. It reminded me of some bizarre scene out of the seventies. Disco lights, streamers, and a giant piñata thrown in for good measure.

"Jesus Christ," I muttered to myself, twitching irritatingly.

"Evie sure has outdone herself this time," Marc bellowed into my ear, the music drowning out most of his praise.

I just smiled. The knot in my stomach tightened at the sound of her name.

Bitch.

Why did I have to be so nice? Why could I not just sock it to him then and there? Because I knew payback was coming and I simply had to wait.

Most of the evening's festivities went by in a haze. I was not really bothered and just sat patiently biding my time.

"You look beautiful," a familiar voice said from behind me.

"Alex!" I smiled, and jumping up, I hugged him tight. "I'm so glad you came. I couldn't do this without you."

"Honey, I would not miss this for anything," he laughed, pulling me closer to him. He slipped the disc into my hand and kissed me on the nose. "Knock them dead!"

Slipping the disc into my purse, I smiled nervously as I looked at Marc acting like a jackass with his friends and knew there was no turning back.

"Before we entertain the masses, how about you loosen up and join me on the dance floor," Alex said as he took me by the hand and twirled me around.

"Alex, I can't dance. You know I can't." I tried to argue with him.

"Don't be silly. I've taught you all you know. Now let's show these fools how it's done." He laughed as he pulled me in closer to him.

I giggled loudly, loud enough to get Marc's unwanted attention. I spun round and shook my ass, almost grinding myself up against Alex, and I did it all to spite Marc.

Looking at Alex as we slowed down and danced to *'Pictures of You'* by The Cure, I examined his face. He was so beautiful and I really could not understand how he had never bothered much with the girls at school. It was always college girls who got the most attention. I knew he was selective with his choices and that he was never short of female company, but sometimes the way he looked at me kind of made me feel all giddy. If things had been different, or if we were in another life, maybe something would have happened between us.

Alex was the closest friend I had. He was everything a girl could want in a guy, tall, toned, mousy blond hair with curls that fell over his face, and the most luscious emerald green eyes. But it just never happened for us. His friendship was precious and I could never complicate it with a crush. *Especially now.*

I do not know what I felt, but God, something inside me almost burst. I pulled away from him, retreated back to my table, and diverted my attention to something, anything, other than him.

The music stopped and Brookes took to the stage, it was time.

The inevitable was about to happen. Marc and I were, after all, the 'it' couple, or, more to the point, I was dating the 'it' guy. So, being crowned prom King and Queen did not surprise me in the slightest. The crowd cheered and applauded as we both made our way to the centre stage.

He high-fived a few of the guys from the football team and waved like he was a film star. I received my crown first. I smiled and waved to a few girls from my class and then stood back as Marc received his crown. I had never really seen him as an ass before now, but seriously, he was parading around the stage like a total retard. I felt like a fraud for the first time ever.

"Wow," he gushed into the mike. "This is something else, and you know what? You guys rock!" he shouted. Everyone, well, almost everyone, cheered and whooped.

"But seriously, my girlfriend rocks. She's made me the guy I am, so give it up for Giselle." He looked back at me with those adorable puppy dog brown eyes and gorgeous cheeky grin that first made me fall for him.

God, I was nervous.

I flipped the disc in my hand and slipped it into the DVD player that Alex had so kindly set up for me earlier. Walking to the front of the stage, I fidgeted nervously. All eyes were on me and, trembling, I removed the crown from my head.

"You know something? I always dreamed of this night. Marc and I standing here, hand in hand, living what every high school couple dream of. This is so cool, seriously, but I kinda have to forfeit this great, honourable prize." I heard the echo of stunned gasps. "I know you all probably think I've gone mad, but I believe that a girl here tonight should be standing where I am instead of me because this girl has earned it, in more ways than one. And for your pleasure, I'd like to introduce you to a match made in heaven."

Clicking play on the remote control, I waited for the penny to drop. I could not stop trembling. The adrenalin was pumping through me and Alex was soon by my side holding my hand. He was my saviour.

Marc was taken aback. He looked at me, confused, and for a split second, I felt sorry for him. On the screen, Evie moaned, moving her hips back and forth. Marc held her ass, sweating as he kissed the nape of her neck. It was pretty obvious what they were doing, but I could not bring myself to look. The noise from the tape drowned out any chatter amongst the crowd, and inside, I felt my heart crumble into a million little pieces.

Looking around, I saw the reactions on people's faces. Some stood with their hands over their mouths. Others

25

laughed, and a few of the football guys cheered, while teachers rushed around trying to find the off switch.

I stood in front of the mike, and exhaled. "I believe that Evie Stokes is the rightful owner of this crown. She has earned it." I dropped the crown on the floor and left the stage.

Concentrating on nothing but the exit sign above the security door, I briskly walked towards it. I had to get out of there and no one was going to stop me. Marc tried to run after me, but Alex thwarted him.

"Let it go, man. She doesn't want to know." Alex pushed Marc back into the crowd.

"It's not what it looks like. Alex, dude, you've got to believe me. You know the truth. Alex, you know what really happened. You gotta help me out, man," Marc pleaded breathlessly.

Alex laughed as he pushed his hair from his eyes. "You know, I'd believe you, only the footage speaks louder than words. Besides, I'm not interested in your sob story."

The noise from the crowd became a mere echo as my tunnel vision led me away from the chaos I had caused, chaos that would one day come back to haunt me.

Chapter 3

Outside, the cold night air hit me hard in the face. I ached inside, and soon, the tears were burning my eyes as I cried hysterically. I ran as far as I could, not stopping until I entered *Round Lake Park*. The dimly lit pathway led me down to the shore of the lake and I crumpled in a heap. I sobbed for what seemed like an eternity, only stopping when the silence around me caught my attention. It was so dark that I could hardly make out the street lamps on *Old Highway 8*. The water rippled gently, silently hitting the stones on the bank. I felt more isolated than ever before.

From the corner of my eye, I could see a dark figure standing there watching me. The silhouette was covered by the low hanging branches of the trees and I could barely make it out.

I froze.

Holding my breath, I looked around me, trying to get my bearings. I knew I had to make a run for it, but the damn dress was so tight and even in bare feet, I probably would not be able to outrun whoever it was.

Fumbling around me in the darkness, my hand found a lump of wood. I grabbed a hold of it tightly and got up. Frantically, I tried to control my breathing.

Come on, Giselle. Get it together!

I studied my opponent. I could not make out his face but he was definitely male and he looked so much bigger than me, although the distance between us was too much for me to be sure. That was when I made the worst mistake of all. I ran like a scared little child. Hitting the overgrowth of the trees with my bare arms, I could feel the sting from the cuts, and in error, I looked down to examine the damage while trying to catch my breath.

Big mistake!

He was right there in front of me. He stood like a tower over me. I could not believe my eyes.

"Alex!" I yelled, flinging myself into his solid chest. His arms wrapped around me, holding me tight.

Right then, in that moment, I felt completely safe.

"How did you know where to find me?" I cried, sniffling as I looked up into his deep green eyes.

Brushing the hair from my chin, he smiled down at me. His voice was smooth and calm. "Because I always know where you are."

I did not see the need to question him, and instead, I closed my eyes tight and relaxed in the embrace, unable to let go. Alex always had a way of calming me. In whatever situation, he would come and rescue me. He was what I needed right now. I wanted to forget about the drama of Marc and Evie. I hated them both. They had hurt me in a way I did not think was possible. Well, not possible from the guy who claimed to love me.

My heart broke.

"You know, I can take all your pain away." Alex spoke softly, almost mesmerizing.

"I don't think even you can do that."

"Giselle, I can safely say that I can change the course your life takes."

"Alex . . ."

He grabbed a hold of my hands and looked hard into my face as an odd sensation pulsated through my head. "If you come willingly, then yes, all the pain and heartache will go and in its place you will have peace," he sighed, looking down at his feet. "I have waited so long for you. You do not know how many times I wanted to tell you the truth, to come clean about who I am."

"What . . . ? What do you mean? Alex, this is all a bit too dramatic, even for you." I looked into his face. It was hard and serious.

From behind, I heard whispers and movement. I looked around and saw three men I had never seen before. They wore black and each had a mark tattooed on his face.

"What's going on, Alex?" There was panic in my voice and for the first time ever, I was afraid of my best friend.

"It is time, Master," the tallest of the men said as his eyes blazed red.

Alex smiled down at me. His eyes gleamed in the light of the moon and the peculiar feeling increased, leaving me dizzy and lightheaded.

"Please, Giselle, come quietly and it will be over quickly."

"The moon, Master. It will enter the second phase and you will have failed."

I had to be dreaming. Jesus, I mean, after all I had been through, it was possibly my mind playing tricks on me. There was no other explanation.

"Quiet!" Alex raised his voice. "Giselle, I have chosen you to be by my side. It is you who will redeem my bloodline, but you must come willingly. I cannot force you, but if you decide against me then I will have to destroy you. We have only a few minutes until the moon changes and our window of opportunity will have passed. Please, I implore you, oblige and you will feel no pain. I do not want to harm you."

"Oh my God, you're all crazy!" I shouted as I tried to fight the inebriating feeling overcoming me.

Trying to back away from the edge of the trees, I made a run for it. It seemed impossible, but Alex moved with stellar speed. I was seriously no match for him, but I gave it my best shot. I hit him hard in the face. He did not move, and in a blink of an eye, he was behind me with his warm, strong hands around my waist, holding me close to him.

"Why are you doing this?"

"Because I must awaken you. Giselle, you do not have a choice." His breath was warm on my neck.

"I don't understand," I whimpered.

"Say yes and all will be revealed. I promise you there will be no pain."

"But . . . I can't. I don't want to die."

"You will not die. You will be reborn."

"But . . . Alex, you're scaring me."

"Giselle, please. I am running out of time and it is you who must join me." His voice became harder.

Not wanting to give in, I tried my best to block out his voice and fight the urge to give in, but the power of his grip and the three men who stood before me told me that I would lose whichever fate I chose.

"Okay . . . No, I don't know . . . Okay," I whispered, nodding my head in defeat as tears streamed down my cheeks.

What was I doing? I screamed inside my head.

No . . . no . . . no . . . please. It was pointless, because soon enough, my thoughts became lost in a daze of smouldering heat.

His breath was warm and velvety as he brushed his lips along my neck. He gently kissed and caressed my throat with his tongue and the sensation sent my skin into overdrive. I was completely spellbound. I found it hard to concentrate and, before long, I was lost in the warmth of his touch. Moving his mouth over mine, I kissed him back. I never imagined his mouth would be so electrifying. His breath was sweet and intoxicated every inch of my body.

His lips left my mouth and found their way down my neck. He opened his mouth wide and bit down. At first, the pain of the bite burned, but I soon found myself lost in its burning pleasure. It was my first experience of ecstasy and then there was nothing, just complete blackness.

* * *

Everywhere around me I could hear voices with unfamiliar soft accents. I was aware of my own faint heartbeat; its weak pulse throbbed and echoed in my head. I felt different. The heat from within me burned like a fire in a furnace. I ached all over and not one inch of my body was spared the torture. I tried to will my eyes open, but nothing would happen. Frustrated, I wanted to scream, but my voice was unheard.

What was happening to me?

Hurried footsteps came to a stop beside me. The gentle touch of a hand rubbed softly against my cheek. All my senses came rushing to me like a ball of heat. I yearned for that touch and the desire for it engulfed me, but still my eyes remained closed.

"She's burning up," he spoke softly.

"The third day is always the worst. She will be whole by moonlight." A hoarse voice reassured him.

"Of course. You are right."

"You are aware that the thirst will be unbearable when she wakes. Are you sure you are ready for the responsibility that comes with awakening a mortal?"

"She is mine. I am ready for whatever comes my way." He was confident, but his voice was sharp with anger.

Oh my God.

As quickly as he came, he was gone from my side, leaving me alone and afraid.

Terrified, I tried to fight the pain, but it overwhelmed me and I succumbed to the burning in my throat. The flames engulfed every vein within my body and my skin felt like it had melted from the heat. I could feel the warm blood ooze from every cavity. I wanted to die.

I prayed for death.

* * *

I awoke to the light of the moon shining bright into my eyes. Voices hushed and I could hear the anticipation in their whispered voices.

"She is seeking us out. This is truly a night for the Goddess," one of them gleefully remarked.

My natural instinct had me on the defensive. I backed away from them. Every cell in my body told me they were dangerous. They were strange and did not look like anything I had seen before. Yet, the back of my throat burned, my chest ached, and dizziness filled my head with so much uncertainty.

Was this all a dream?

"Giselle." A name, my name, was called.

I turned my head, ready to pounce. I thought I knew him. He seemed familiar, but I still could not trust him. Something in his voice did not seem right.

"Who are you?" I spoke, but my voice was not my own any more. Coughing, I tried to clear my throat, failing to get rid of the deep burning.

He stood beside me. Reaching out his hand, he waited for me to respond. I retreated. I did not trust this stranger. His eyes seemed sad, yet knowingly he brushed the hair from my face, leaving my burning eyes vulnerable to the moonlight.

"Giselle, my love, you must feed in order to complete the transition." His eyes were fixed on mine and for a moment, I thought I felt a connection.

"I want to go. I do not belong here," I angrily snapped at him, squinting hard as I tried to shield my eyes from the light.

He tried to touch my arm, but I caught him within my grip and instinct had me ready to kill him. Yet something about his smell stopped me. I knew that sweet scent, but could not place it.

I looked deep within his eyes, staring intently until some kind of memory came to me. He paused too, touching my lips with his fingertips. I knew that touch, that soft skin against my feverishly hot flesh and he calmed something within me. I did know him. It was becoming clearer to me now.

Oh God, it was him, I remembered. It was Alex.

"You did this to me," I wailed, pulling back from him. "You chose."

"No. You forced me into this! I never had a choice," I hissed at him and stared at those around me.

I became more aware of my surroundings. I was in a room, built with marble and at the far left stood a monument of an ancient queen. Around her feet were fresh flowers entwined with ivy, thorns, and fresh orchids. A large oak table stood dead centre in the room. On top of it, books and scrolls were scattered. On the walls hung giant portraits of people and scary looking shadows, and a familiar face stood out from the rest, Alex.

"You must drink."

"Oh no! There is no way on this earth I am going to do that." I rejected him as the thirst burned inside me.

"Giselle, you have to drink. If you do, you will start to heal." He used his most persuasive voice.

I shook my head in protest. "I can't. I'm not like you. I want to go. Please, let me go home. Please," I begged.

He used a sharp dagger and cut deep into his wrist. The sweet smell instantly caught my attention and the burning desire rose within me. I found myself moving my mouth closer to his wrist and with one last try at abstaining, I gave in and let the blood fill my mouth.

Alex closed his eyes and gently smiled as I drank. I gulped down his sweet blood. Its syrupy texture slid along my throat, electrifying every corner of my body. I had never imagined anything like it. I wanted to continue, only to be disturbed by someone pulling my head away.

"Enough. You will weaken him if you do not stop," a man's voice echoed in my ear.

"Enough!"

I pulled away, gasping sharply. I felt disgusted with myself for drinking from him, the thought of his blood running through me made me shake violently. Alex had his eyes closed tight as his breathing laboured. He did not notice me practically convulsing next to him. An eerie silence filled the room as I just sat and watched him smile.

"The first drink is always the ice-breaker," Alex laughed as he closed his eyes again.

"The first?" I asked, stunned. "Do I have to do this more than once?"

An old woman interrupted. She ushered me out of the way and tended to Alex's wound. One lick from the tip of her tongue and the cut sealed itself, and any sign of my feeding from him was gone.

"You are blood bound. You must drink from your regnant on three separate nights to fulfill your bond," she said calmly as she walked towards the door.

"I don't understand," I complained. "This is all too much. Why me?"

"Giselle, you were chosen for me by my elders," he spoke softly as his eyes remained closed.

I sighed and sat beside him. "Am I dead?" I innocently asked him.

"No, I merely bit and awakened you. Your heart still beats and your blood still runs warm and red. Only your basic instincts have changed. You will feed from me and me alone. You will not have to kill for your food and in return, I will feed from you and our blood bond will grow. Good things will happen because of you." He sounded so confident.

He took a deep breath and silently rested.

I could not answer. Everything was happening too fast and my mind found it hard to accept what I was hearing. I mean, how could I? I did not even know what I had become. I sunk my head into my knees, unable to cry. I craved the normality of a high school betrayal.

I wanted to run. I wanted to escape this craziness and I did not want to hear any of it. This was not my Alex talking. It was some impostor playing a cruel joke on me.

I watched the men at work around me, trying hard to ignore their strange features. Their purplish dark skin sat tight against their bodies and their long tangled hair was worn loose around their shoulders. Their deep red eyes were the most startling of all. They seemed to be devoid of life, cold and hollow. They wore the same black clothing, each resembling the other except for the emblem on each cheek. The symbol was unique, each one slightly different to the other. The man nearest to me had a black dagger with an oval head shaded in crimson on his right cheek, the centre of the dagger engraved with tiny letters. I could not make out the wording, but the intrinsic art was beautiful.

I was caught staring and hid my face. Within a second, he stood there in front of me with eyes that were wide and frightening.

"What is it you seek, child?" He brushed his hand across my face.

I refused to respond. His breath was sharp and enticing and I found myself becoming weaker and unable to resist looking into his eyes. The red pools rippled seductively. I wanted to swim deep within him, and for a moment, I lost my senses and aimed forward.

He laughed.

"You have a lot to learn, dearest Giselle. My blood is not for your taking." He cackled as he pushed me hard against the wall. I was paralysed. My body was rigid. I couldn't move an inch.

I was trapped.

Alex, wake up, I mouthed, but no words left my mouth.

"Do not be frightened. I merely feel that you have been left uneducated." He turned his back on me and reached for something on the table.

Every eye in the room was on me now and Alex was slowly coming around and becoming aware of what was happening. He rose to his feet and walked over to me.

"Afanas, what is the meaning of this? Release her at once!"

Afanas sighed. "The girl has been ill informed and I believe she must fully understand what is expected of her. Alexander, I apologize." He bowed his head.

Released, I fell to the ground in a heap and looked up at Alex as he offered me his hand. I took it and he helped me to my feet. He exhaled and gestured for me to follow him.

Outside, the air was thin and icy. I felt the cold, but did not shiver. We walked in silence until we stopped at an old fountain. The water flowed with brilliance as the moonlight sparkled brightly on my reflection.

"Giselle, I do not pretend to think that any of this is easy. To be honest, I didn't think I would pull it off." Stopping, he looked at me. He pushed the hair back from my ear and smiled. "I've known you for almost six years and not once have I been totally honest with you." His voice changed.

"Alex, you're scaring me. You have no idea how frightened I am."

"My birth name is Alexander Baranski, not Alex Burns like you thought. I am the son of Prince Leonid Baranski." He paused.

I shook my head. "No, this doesn't make sense. I've known you since we were twelve-years-old. Surely, I would have noticed something different in you." I tried hard not to cry.

"My family is a descendent of the Nelapsi. We are not gluttons like them, as we can survive quite well on small amounts of blood, but we need to add to our bloodline for the sake of our future. A future that involves you."

I could not take much more. I did not want to believe any of this. It was nonsense, yet he seemed so sincere.

"I want to go home right now. Take me home, Alex, please," I begged him. Tears welled up in my eyes, burning as I held them back.

"Don't you understand what I'm telling you? You can never go back, not until the prophecy has been fulfilled." His voice was tense. "Giselle, what you knew as life has changed. You will become one of us. It something that has already begun and there is no way of reversing it. You must accept this as your fate. Don't fight it."

"What God-damned prophecy? What the hell have I become, Alex, huh? What am I, if I'm not dead?" I screamed into his face.

"A nightwalker; a vampire."

Chapter 4

The words stunned me and I was rendered speechless. I looked around me, reeling from the word used to describe my newfound fate. This had to be some sick and cruel joke.

Vampire.

Holy mother of hell. Alex was much more messed up than I thought. I mean, in this day and age, we've all heard the same old stories over and over again, but that did not mean I had to believe it. Vampires did not exist and that was something I was sure of.

He stopped my train of thought and hesitated before he spoke. "Giselle, say something, anything."

"You are so out of your frigging mind," I said as I moved away from him.

He forced me to stand still and held his hands upon my shoulders. "Look at me, Giselle. Really look at me. What do you see?"

I stared at him, looking at his beautiful green eyes and the loose blond curls that fell around them. He was a stunning sight to behold. His high chiselled cheekbones would make any guy jealous and his body was rippled, yet so soft. But it was his eyes that held me, the green turning a reddish-brown. Slowly, a crimson red overflowed from them and then I saw the same blood that I had seen within Afanas's.

I stepped back from him. "You . . . Your eyes."

"I'm sorry," he choked, turning his back on me as he walked further away.

I could not believe what I was seeing. The guy who had saved me from every pitfall, who helped wipe my tears whenever Marc let me down, this same guy was a monster. I could not comprehend what I was seeing or hearing. At that precise moment, I felt something inside me. It wasn't my emotions; I could feel someone else's torment The shame at what he had done, but mixed up with that combination of guilt, I sensed something deeper, something that frightened me, something that was both hate and disgust. I tried my best to forget I had felt it. I looked at Alex as he slowly faced me and it was then I knew the so called bond had begun.

Suddenly, the urge to hold him overcame me, I couldn't fight the repulsion at what he had done to me and I found myself embracing him. I had no control over my actions. It was as though something had taken over my body, but I knew that deep down inside, I wanted to hold him. *Or that was how I thought I felt.*

It was his eyes that held the truth. They were cold and distant and it was not the Alex I had known or come to love. I wanted him to be sorry. I wanted the old Alex back, not this thing I felt compelled to hold.

"Am I really a vampire?" I muttered in his ear.

"Yes, but a new breed."

"I don't understand. What makes me different?" I said, feeling completely crushed.

"You will remain mortal. Well, almost."

"Err, I just don't get it!"

"Giselle, your soul never left your body. You remain alive. Only your humanity is slightly altered."

I gave him the same puzzled look I had worn since I had awoken.

"Okay. When I bit you, I drank from you, and whilst doing the deed, I kind of tainted your blood with my venom. Not enough to kill you, but enough to kick-start a change. Kind of like a metamorphosis, if you like. You know, a mutation of your DNA."

"Right, so I'm not dead. I'm still human, only kinda like a mutant? That figures!"

He laughed at me. "Yeah, a mutant, only you need blood and certain life forces to sustain you."

He arched his right eyebrow and gave me that million dollar smile of his. I was such a sucker for that smile.

"Life forces?" I said, puzzled.

"You will need the life force of humans to survive. You will drink their souls."

"*Oh my God,*" I cried.

"Giselle . . ." he started, only to have me cut him off.

"Will I ever see my family again?" I felt heartbroken, thinking about my erratic, but loveable, mother.

"You can see them, but from a distance. It would be too dangerous for them."

"But if I'm not like you, then how can I be any danger to them?"

"It is not you who would be any threat to them. It would be the rogue vampires hunting you, amongst other things."

"What?" I exclaimed.

"You are going to be hot property, Giselle. In order for us to keep you safe, I'm afraid that all contact with the outside world will have to cease until after you have been consecrated."

"But they'll be worried! You know what Mom is like. She'll probably have the FBI searching for me right now. God, what if they're freaking out?" I cried, and then asked, "Consecrated?"

Alex held my hand. "Look at me. All has been taken care of. You left town to get yourself together after being deceived by Marc. You'll keep in contact via the phone and you'll call in every week or so. You've reassured them that you won't do anything crazy and the consecration *thing* is a simple blessing done by the elders."

"It seems like every angle has been covered. Except, I feel kinda left out. I'm the one who's been expected to just take all of this on the chin and accept it for what it is. It's so unfair, Alex. You should have been honest with me from the beginning. Marc's deception hasn't got a thing on yours!"

Pushing him away, I walked back towards the path, feeling completely destroyed. I wished I would wake up from this nightmare that was now my so called 'life.' I wanted to look back, but my stubbornness refused to let me give in to my newly forged bond.

* * *

The moon was partially covered by lingering clouds that seemed to follow me. I walked the length of the path to a clearing and entered a small courtyard. Up until then, I had not taken notice of my surroundings and realised I was no longer in Minnesota. The sweet scent of the blossoms hit my nose and for the first time ever, I inhaled the delicious fragrance and absorbed its beauty. My senses were now much more acute.

Opening my eyes, I saw a beautiful woman approaching me. Her long red hair blew effortlessly in the still of the night. Her eyes were deep red, her lips full and her complexion whiter than snow.

"Giselle Bergman, it is an honour and a privilege to meet you," she said as she held out her arms to me.

I had no clue who she was, but I felt obligated to allow her to embrace me.

"The night is our time, the time for understanding, chimera and meditation. The darkness we see now covers the earth. Our hearts are whole. Now, the night is ours," she sang in my ear.

Whatever she said was way above my head and I just smiled in confused appreciation.

She laughed as she let go of me, raising her hands up in the air. "Giselle, there is no need to be afraid. I am Alexander's nevlastná matka, or step-mother, Atarah." She laughed as she watched my every move.

"Oh, hi," I muttered awkwardly.

Alex had not once mentioned *her,* only his father Leo. How stupid I felt.

"Walk with me, child."

"I'm sorry if I seem rude, but tonight has been kind of surreal."

"But, of course. You have undergone some magnificent, but all the same terrifying changes. I would not expect you to feel anything other than scared. It's natural, but rest assured you are with those who have your best interest at heart." She spoke softly, calming the nerves that had knotted in the pits of my stomach.

The noticeable burning began in the back of my throat, and instantly, I yearned for blood. I became agitated and I was pretty sure that my face said it all.

"Giselle, are you all right?"

"I don't know," I panicked. "I don't know what's happening to me."

Suddenly, I was out cold, lying on the bitter frosty ground. I was unconscious for but a moment, but Alex was soon by my side.

I felt so weak and unsure of my feelings. I wanted to wake up from the madness of this nightmare, but something deep within tried to reason with me, convincing me of its truth. I knew what was happening, but I was in denial. I wanted to forget about the present and slip into the past, a place where life was ordinary and I was not expected to be something other than myself.

* * *

"Giselle, don't even think about peeking, ok?" Marc teased as he led me through a doorway.

Laughing, I could not help but feel completely in love with him. It was early September, the beginning of our final year of school, and life truly could not get any better. Marc was always very spontaneous with his gestures of love and tonight was no exception.

"I'm not." I giggled like a little girl.

One final step and we stood still. The excitement was getting the best of me and I slowly opened my eyes.

"Oh Marc," I said in amazement.

The Porter & Frye, the most luxurious restaurant in town, was empty except for two waiters who smiled exuberantly as Marc led me to a table laid with rose petals. Candles were lit and filled the empty tables around us. It was utterly romantic and I melted into his arms.

"I love you so much," I whispered as I tenderly kissed him.

"Easy, tiger," he teased me.

"So, why all this? Not that I'm complaining."

"Can't a guy do something for the woman he loves without there being an ulterior motive?"

"Well, you tell me." I folded my arms and waited for his perfect smile to spread across his face.

I could not stop smiling. I swear my jaw ached, but it was impossible to stop. A waiter approached us and handed us a menu.

"Okay, here's the thing. We're approaching the end of an era. You know, school and all, and I don't want us to forget about the reasons we're together. It's you, and it's always been you, and I refuse to let you forget that for a second. You're my girl, G, and nothing is going to change that. Plus, my dad was owed a favour and pulled a few strings." He playfully winked at me.

Marc had a way with words and as we both laughed, my heart was almost ready to burst with the incredible feelings I had towards him. I was completely in love with him.

I found it hard to resist. I was his. The hottest guy at school was mine and nothing would get in the way of that. Ever.

* * *

The agony I felt was unbearable. My head spun in circles and I found it hard not to wail. I saw Alex's face as he sat by my side, the frown on his brow giving away his worry.

"She needs to feed." Atarah directed Afanas to the table.

He bowed his head and was gone in a flash, returning with a dagger in his hand that he held out to Alex.

"Can we at least have some privacy this time?" His voice broke as he spoke to his mother.

"Of course, if that is your will."

Atarah raised her hand to Alex's face and stroked his chin. He closed his eyes and soon she and Afanas were gone, leaving Alex alone with me.

I sat up, trying not to lose my balance. My head was still light from the emptiness. With the dagger in his hand, he cut deeply into his neck, leaving a stream of thick scarlet flowing from the wound. The aroma was tantalizing and I could not resist.

Swiftly, I was on top of him, straddling his lap. I licked the line of blood and desire burned deep within us both. He pulled me closer to him, his hands firmly placed on my back. My mouth opened wider and with voracity, I drank.

I could feel Alex's excitement as it swept through him, his blood awakening every cell in my body. The mutual lust we shared was something I had never experienced before. It made the transition all the more easier.

If fate had played a part in this, then maybe I would adjust. Given time, I would learn to accept my role in my new life.

Maybe.

Chapter 5

My head was still spinning from the rush when a tall man with dark short hair came to my side. He looked down at both Alex and I. He did not speak. He stared until his attention was stirred by Atarah's arrival. She looked angelical, her beauty like nothing I had ever seen before. Her deep brown eyes held the same allure as Alex's and I found it hard not to gasp when they changed momentarily, a deep red flushing away the charisma.

I felt as though I was part of a freak show with the blood fresh on my lips leaving me exposed. Anger welled up inside me and I wanted to scream. I did not understand the constant intrusions. So much was happening too fast and I wanted to slow down.

Alex wiped his neck as he stood up and then he reached for my hand and helped me to my feet. I looked at him, waiting for some kind of explanation, only to be faced with silence.

Atarah broke the obvious tension. "Do not be alarmed by Leonid's presence. He was eager to meet you, Giselle."

I looked at the large man standing in front of me. His eyes were unlike Alex's. They were cold and mean. He was undoubtedly beautiful, his well-formed body and his face were picture perfect. I never imagined Alex's father to be so young and attractive. I blushed at my thoughts, convinced that everyone would know what I was thinking.

"Father," Alex said through gritted teeth.

"Alexander, I believe there is much excitement surrounding your new mate. However, I'm concerned that you have been neglecting your own well-being by allowing her to feed so ravenously from you."

Leonid eyed me disapprovingly and I wanted to curl up and cry like a baby. There was something disconcerting about his presence, and it didn't help the already tense situation.

"Father, it was I who insisted that she feed from me. I do not like the thought of her relying on other sources. I am fine," Alex snapped back.

"I think you misunderstand me. I forbid you to be her only source. You have a glamorised vision that the pair of you can feed off of each other without consequences." He paced back and forth, his eyes darkening with anger.

Alex walked past his mother with clenched fists. "You cannot forbid something that is already at work. I can feel our bond strengthening, and by the next full moon, Giselle will have completed the third phase and will be my mate. We will share the blood oath and we will be equals." Alex smiled at me, his fangs glistening in the dimly lit room.

Leonid laughed raucously. "Son, you have much to learn. She is a new breed of vampire, one whose heart still beats. She, unlike you, cannot withstand the blood loss. Remember that she is unaware of her true desires. Spiritual vampires desire the life energy of their victims. The blood is just a bonus. You risk much more than your own existence. Her creation is for the future of our kind, not just as your soul mate. You will do as I say. That is my final word on the matter." He finished, momentarily glancing over at me as he left the room.

I could feel Alex's anger as he flipped the table over. In all the time I had known him, I had never seen so much rage. He scared me. This was not the boy who I had considered to be my best friend; *this* was something else. Standing with my back against the wall, I did not dare move. I just watched as he tore the room apart.

Atarah turned her back on him and looked me in the eye. "It is times like this when you realise that the animal still lurks deep within one's heart. He does not command the experience to control his raw emotions. He is young, like you, and has yet to learn that things cannot be rushed. You will do as Leonid instructed, but if you were to, let's say, offer yourself to Alexander, he might see things differently. Your blood might rationalize his displeasure," she whispered as she placed a finger over her lips.

Choking on my own saliva, I swallowed hard. *Offer myself to Alex?* God, I did not want to use some dagger to cut myself or, worse, let him bite me. Hell, I didn't want to see my own blood. It grossed me out.

Leaving the room, Atarah looked back at me and winked. It was a surreal moment. I could not believe that she wanted me to ignore Leonid's orders and let Alex feed from me.

Crap.

Alex was still breathing hard as I approached him. His eyes were a deep red colour and his hair was wet with sweat. "Alex," I started, my voice shaking. "Please stop. You're kinda scaring the hell out of me, and . . ."

"Giselle, please, just don't."

He hurried out of the room. I ran after him into the cool air. Sunrise was approaching and the blue haze of morning was mixed with orange. I did not know if it was possible for me to be outside, and then I remembered, *Alex never shied away from the sun back home.* I thought vampires were afraid of the sunlight?

A tinge of excitement ran through me as I called after him. "Alex, wait."

Ignoring me, he walked faster, all the while clenching his fists.

"Alex, would you cut this out? I'm tired and I haven't got a clue as to what the hell is happening here. Please!"

He stopped and turned to face me. "Giselle, I'm afraid my father is right. You cannot rely on me. You're not strong enough to withstand the blood loss."

"Hold up. You said that we'd feed only off each other. Why the sudden change of heart?"

"Because I was being selfish. I wanted you to myself and I was wrong." His voice saddened, but his eyes remained glazed and cold.

"I don't get it. I mean, all that stuff you said earlier, was that just bullshit?"

"Of course not. We will be bound by blood. But Giselle, I'm not sure I've explained what will become of us."

"Then tell me, please!"

The morning light began to shine through the canopy of the trees, its amber glow a welcome sight. Birds began to sporadically sing their morning song, and for a split second, it was a beautiful sight.

We sat amongst the trees, the beam of light illuminating Alex's pale skin.

"For centuries, vampires have co-existed with different lairs, each one abiding by ancient rules. Unfortunately, my family have been subjected to centuries of disrespect and violence. The Nelapsi, our mother herd, was responsible for sowing the seeds of chaos amongst our people, resulting in a revolt among the elders. Many chose different paths. Others abdicated their birthright. Do you follow?"

I nodded my head, a little confused, but nonetheless interested.

"The elders believe that a child born from the union of a male vampire and female human will result in a change of heart among the Kindred. It would dispel any rumour concerning our attitude towards humans. We are *not* our ancestors."

"Err, how can I . . . I mean, I'm not ready for babies, never mind life as a vampire-come-human. I mean, how can we? You're like soulless, right?" I asked, frustrated.

"Yes, I'm soulless and slightly different, but all my 'boy bits' work exactly like any other guy out there."

Oh my God! We were actually having this conversation.

"If that's the case, why did you bite me in the first place?"

"Because if you were to carry my child you would need the sustenance of another source. Your human body alone would not be enough for the unborn. My venom was enough to kick-start the transition and nothing more."

"Oh great, so I'm to be some kind of glorified incubator?"

Alex knelt in front of me, not giving me time to respond. "Giselle, you are much more than that. You are everything to me and I only wish you could feel the same way. I know that you will never love me the way you loved Marc, but given time, I believe that you can learn to offer me something in return."

"Alex, I can't see me doing this. I don't know how I'm meant to understand any of this. I'm just an ordinary girl, with simple dreams. This life . . . it's wrong."

"You have no other choice. We are obligated to produce and that is something that cannot be changed."

Sometimes, when I get angry, I feel the urge to scream and yell like some crazed woman from one of those Hammer horror movies. Now was one of those times.

Not holding back, I punched him hard in the face. I had caught him off guard and he fell back slightly, but I was really no match for him and in seconds, he had me defeated. I lay on the ground with his heavy torso on mine, his face inches from mine. I refused to look him in the eye.

"If you're going to bite me, just get it over with," I provoked him through gritted teeth.

Alex moved his face closer to mine, placing his free hand on my throat. He tightened his grip and kissed me firmly on the lips. I tried not to respond but temptation got the better of me. I found myself drowning in the warmth of his kiss, the air between us becoming thinner, and something more intense took over my body. I pulled him closer to me, drawing my leg up against his thigh. I could feel every inch of his body pressing against mine. I was so turned on that I forgot about my anger and let myself go. Running my fingers through his hair, my tongue passionately caressed his lips and my nails ran roughly down his bare back, I hadn't even noticed him removing it.

Alex did not give me a chance to breathe. He moved his mouth closer to my neck, biting down sharply, leaving me gasping from the mixture of pain and pleasure. The rush that soon followed was more intense than the first time he bit me. This was pure joy. I could feel him grinding hard against me, and soon I reached a climax that left my entire body shaking. I was completely exhilarated. I was on a high.

***

The next few hours, I slept contently dreaming about Alex and how he made me feel. I never thought it possible to feel so much lust and anger for someone. I could not think of one other time I had let desire take over. I always had so much control when I was alone with Marc. I did not know if the new me was something I would learn to love or hate, the latter being the obvious choice.

Guilt built up, and soon I was awake, staring at the ceiling and thinking of Marc. I felt as though I had just betrayed him, as if it was I who had done the dirty deed and cheated on him. I envied my innocence and longed for my old life.

They say that when we take revenge against another, we lose some of our innocence. Maybe this was my retribution, and if it was, then God had a very sick way of making me pay.

* * *

Feeling restless, I found it hard to sleep, so I got up and decided to make myself a little decent, something which had not occurred since prom. I was not expecting my reflection to startle me. I looked like me, but there was certainly some kind of change going on. My once olive complexion was gone, and in its place was a subtler glow, a luminescence.

The colour of my dark brown eyes remained the same. My lips were a little plumper, but it was the dark circle in the hollow of my chest that frightened me. I rubbed hard to remove the stain, but it refused to shift and remained there; a darkness between my breasts.

I cried.

This change wasn't what I wanted. I wanted to remain the same, and if Alex was right about my soul, then why did things have to change? Why did I have to leave everything behind me for some crazy vampire war?

Why had I not been given a choice?

I pulled on the nearest sweater and jeans combo I could find and rushed out. The late afternoon sun hit me hard in the face and the gentle heat flowed over my body. I craved it. I loved being out in the light of day and nothing was happening. Content that I was not about to burst into flames or turn to dust, I headed in the direction of the valley.

The steep walk down was harder than I had expected. I fell a few times, losing my feet in the hidden potholes. I passed a series of paths up to the left of the slopes, but as far as I could see they led nowhere. Shuffling on, I soon came to a picturesque stone bridge spanning the width of the stream below. I stopped and rested, taking in the wonderful beauty that surrounded me. I felt at peace as I sat in the silence. No demands, just me and nature.

I sat back and watched the rays of the sun dance among the branches of the willow trees and looked at the large, overgrown roots that were home to a nest of ants. After a while, I considered heading back to the house, but it was so pleasant and so comfortable, that I decided to sit there quietly for a while longer.

The evening sun began to dim and the birds hurried home to their nests with food in their mouths for the young. My stomach rumbled. Food was definitely a good idea.

I got to my feet and headed back toward the slopes. The water in the stream followed me as I made my way across the bridge. For the first time in what seemed like forever, my mind was clear of drama, no Alex, no Marc - bliss!

Sunset happened a lot quicker than I thought it would and with looming darkness at my back, I rushed back up the hill. Momentarily, I forgot my way and stumbled over the root of a tree.

"Crap!" I spat as I fell.

I had only grazed the tip of my elbow, but it stung like hell. Wasting no more time, I picked up my pace and scrambled back up the steep slope, trying hard not to fall victim to any more heather covered holes. I was close to the top when a blast of wind hit me, knocking me flat on my back.

Trying hard to regain my composure, I became increasingly aware of the shadows surrounding me, not one but six of them. With glowing eyes, their black silhouettes moved closer to me with their arms stretched out trying to grab a hold of me. I could feel their hatred, their anger, and most of all, I sensed their desire to harm me. One leapt on top of me, using its nails to dig at the centre of my chest. It drew blood and I screamed, my voice echoing as my heart thumped hard.

This was it. This was how I was going to die.

Chapter 6

Out of nowhere, Leonid landed heavily on the ground. Grabbing me within his arms, he leapt through the rest of the clearing, not stopping until we reached the boundaries of the house.

He set me down gently. His strong arms were smooth, his skin was radiant, and for a moment, his eyes were not dark and cold. They were full of concern and worry.

"You must never leave the boundaries of the estate again."

"I didn't know I was under house arrest," I snapped like a child.

"Must you be so insubordinate?"

"Well, I didn't know it was like some big deal to go for a walk. Next time, I'll check in with the warden," I stuttered.

"Dare you mock me?" He towered over me. His eyes were mean and angry and I swear I could hear his fists clench. "Those shadow-creatures lurk around these boundaries. They are aware of the changes and they do not like the thought of a mortal at work within the lair. Tempt them again and you will be done for."

"Why would they want me? I'm just an ordinary girl, or I was."

"You bear the mark of darkness. It surrounds you. Your soul is tainted and, in time, the darkness will want its reward."

"Meaning what?"

He walked past me without responding and disappeared into the night.

I shouted after him, yelling into the night sky, "Meaning what? I want answers, do you hear me? I want answers!"

Nothing.

"What an ass," I mumbled as I walked through the courtyard. Sometimes my mouth got the best of me, and at the best of times, trying to control the verbal diarrhea was not a pretty sight.

"You friggin' loser," I bellowed into the darkness.

Control, Giselle. Think control.

Easier said than done when you have no idea of what is happening and your stomach is crying out for food, 'real' food.

The old Gothic style building that stood before me was, without a doubt incredible, but it gave me the creeps. Pointed arches and vaults were visible on the windows and doors with steeply pitched gables and balanced thrusts in some of the stone masonry. Stone gargoyles sat on each corner of the roof, their eyes staring down as if they were watching me. Not having noticed it before made me feel very out of the loop.

There I was, *wherever that might be*, alone, with no friends, no crazy mother, and certainly no adoring boyfriend to take that sense of danger away from me.

The shadow-creatures still hung in my head as I walked into the front hall. My skin crawled from fright and the wound on my chest stung. My mind was in another place when I bumped into a woman reading some sort of old book, sending it crashing to the floor.

I casually blurted out, "Sorry about that," as I picked it up.

Unable to the read the strange language of the writing in the book, I handed it back to her. She was old. Her hair was black with silver strands, her eyes were the darkest black and the left one was lazy. Her face was a mass of lines and her teeth gleamed in the light as she smiled at me.

Without giving her time to say anything, I rushed past her down the hall and went through the first door I could find. Old ladies gave me the heebie-jeebies at the best of times, especially ones with fangs, and right then, I did not fancy talking rubbish with another vamp.

"Giselle, what a surprise." Turning around, I saw Afanas sitting at a large table.

"Yep, that's me, full of surprises," I awkwardly responded.

He got up from his chair and walked over to me. His freakish looks did not make me feel any safer and I wanted to run back out the way I came.

"Don't be frightened. Please, sit with me a while." He pointed to a large, comfortable looking couch and I sat down obediently.

"I was looking for the kitchen. I didn't mean to intrude."

He laughed the same sinister laugh I had heard from him before, making my skin crawl.

"The kitchen?" He looked at me as though I was mad.

"Yeah, I'm kinda starving. You know, stomach ache from hunger."

There it was again, that horrid laugh. "But, of course, you are hungry. It has been a long four days. Come, we shall find you lots of nice things to eat."

Well, as surprises go, it was a good one. I could not believe the amount of food I saw in the refrigerator. Meats, cheeses, fresh fruit, bread, chocolate éclairs, (my personal favourite), and, of course, cans of soda. I got stuck into one of the best sandwiches ever. Afanas spread the mustard on thickly, not leaving much bread to show. The ham was delicious and the tomatoes were mouth-wateringly juicy. All was washed down with a gulp of coke.

Heaven.

Afanas watched me intently.

"What?" I asked, feeling quite uncomfortable.

"It gives me great satisfaction seeing you eat," he smirked.

I was totally weirded-out by this. I mean, was he some kind of old letch who got off on young girls eating?

Gross.

"I was hungry."

"Yes, I'm aware of that. My Lord was right about your appetite. However, I didn't quite believe that you would need all this after feeding from him last evening."

Urgh, the blood thing. Why did he have to remind me?

"Yeah, about that. Can we have a conversation where the subject doesn't involve the red stuff?"

"Absolutely. What would you like to talk about?"

Sitting beside me, he observed me as I swallowed the last mouthful.

"Where am I?"

"Ah, well, that is an easy one. We're in the mountains of Utmish Ato-tem."

"Right, and that is where, exactly?"

"Armenia."

Jesus Christ, I was on the other side of the world. Not good, not good at all. Of all the places in the world to be stuck in, Alex had chosen Armenia. I guess I was not too surprised that he had flown me halfway around the world, unconscious and without any ramifications. How the hell he had done it, I did not know, but I promised myself that one day I would get the answers I wanted.

Maybe.

My head ached from all the thinking I was doing. I wanted to call home so badly, but was scared of hearing my mother. I did not know what to expect, so I pushed the longing to the back of my mind and thought of one person only.

Alex.

I had not seen him since last night and I was feeling kind of ashamed of myself. I enjoyed every bit of our encounter, but something made me feel very uneasy about it. It made me feel cheap and whore-like, but still, it was hard trying to ignore the craving inside.

Afanas did not make it any easier. He was trying his best to give me the answers I wanted, but I got the impression he was holding back on me and I hate liars.

"Ok, why here? Why Armenia?

He shuffled uneasily upon the stool. "Because Armenia is our home, our safe haven away from the dangers of more sinister lairs. Here, we are free from harm."

"I still don't get why other vampires would want to harm you. Besides, Alex, I mean Alexander, survived quite well back home. No one ever tried anything on him, did they?"

I could not help put push on.

"Yes, Alexander survived, but that was because of the great lengths his father went to, to protect him. And there was the odd occasion that his life was put in jeopardy."

"Oh, okay. I suppose you are trying your best here, but could you at least elaborate a little more!" I was becoming irritated with the short answers. I wanted more. I needed more.

"Well, hasn't it become quite obvious that we aren't the monsters that folklore portrays us to be?"

"How do you mean?"

"Consider how I could have ripped your throat out and drank you dry. Instead, I sit here and amuse you with my answers. There is a war and you play a vital role. You should have realised by now that you are a very important commodity among vampires. You possess what others seek and it is you who will strengthen the bloodline. We will evolve because of you."

"Yeah, so Alex keeps telling me, but I can't help but wonder how this whole mess started. Why are all of you so afraid of the Nelapsi or whatever they're called?"

He pondered this before he spoke, looking at me intently as though he was about to reveal some deadly secret, and then he began his story.

"I was born more than two centuries ago in a small village called Zemplin in eastern Slovakia. I am what you would call a classical vampire. I am not dead or undead. I just exist. I am what I am. But, of course, my kin the Nelapsi are viscous, bloodthirsty monsters that stop at nothing in order to feed. They care not for their donors. In fact, in most cases, they consume blood with or without permission. It was in the winter of 1790 and times were harsh. Humans were dying from starvation and, as you can imagine, when you rely solely on the blood of a human, it becomes a risk for you when they are dying.

"Unfortunately, that didn't stop many of my brothers. Instead of trying to help them, many turned on the young and defenceless, feeding and consuming their short innocent lives. I couldn't live with that guilt and hated seeing the bloodshed. That is when I found Leonid who helped me and many of my brothers to change what once was an acceptable way of life and we found a new way of co-existing with humans."

"But I thought Leonid was a descendent of the Nelapsi?" I asked, confused.

"Ah, you are right. His majesty is a descendent through birth. He, like Alexander, is an inheritor. Meaning, they were born into their lifestyle like me, but they are not immortal. They can live for a long time, but death does come eventually."

"So, if I wanted to, I could kill them. I mean hurt them?" I stuttered.

He laughed menacingly. "I doubt you would survive long enough to cause them any kind of wound."

I didn't have the balls to answer him back, so we sat in silence. And, of course, being reminded of how he could kill me sent a shiver down my spine, and not in a good way.

Minutes passed before either of us spoke. I was not sure that what he had told me was a good or bad thing. In fact, I was pretty sure I was out of my depth and I did not like the thought of being referred to as a 'commodity.'

"I think I've heard enough. Do you, um, know where Alex is?"

He smiled that same creep-you-out smile he'd had before. "I believe he's resting, but I dare say you'll find him in his room. West wing, top of the stairs, third door on the left."

"Thanks." I smiled as I picked up my can of coke and all but ran from the room.

The hall was barely lit and eerily quiet with only the faint hum of electricity. My pounding heart was making enough noise in my ears to add to the feeling of unease and then a large clock at the top of the stairs began chiming. I ran up the stairs, two steps at a time, and tried not to take any notice of the freaky portraits that hung on the walls. Their eyes just seemed to follow me, as though they knew what I felt inside. Dark pits of nothingness watched me as I stood still.

Pausing at the top, I saw the third door on the left and held my breath as I slowly walked over to it, and knocked gently. There was no answer.

A part of me wanted to turn away and just forget about it. But in a way, I was missing him. Crazy, I know, but it was as though something inside me took over the logical side and turned me into this needy '*thing.*' I wanted to see him badly.

Taking a deep breath, I turned the handle and entered his room. Soft warm light welcomed me as I closed the door. I could hear Alex's gentle breathing as he slept. As I carefully walked over to the side of the bed, I could not help but stare at his naked body. He lay there, still and gorgeous. I could feel my heart beat hard against my chest. I had never seen a naked guy in the flesh before, never mind being alone with one. His chest rose gently with every breath and his eyes moved lightly, dreaming.

For one thing, I was confused. I found it hard to believe that he could be a monster, and yet look so bloody divine and every bit human. From everything I'd ever read or watched, vampires just didn't sleep, breathe, or dream for that matter. This was getting crazier by the second, but the constant pull towards him was so overpowering, I just couldn't resist.

I could feel the flush of my cheeks spreading down the back of my neck and oddly, I found myself becoming more and more aroused with provocative thoughts running through my mind. What went through my head embarrassed me and I found it hard to separate lust from need. I closed my eyes and willed myself to banish them. They refused to leave.

Becoming more aware of my own heavy breathing, I felt his hand against my leg. Opening my eyes, I saw him sleepily smiling at me, the green pools just gazing at me, sucking me further into the cesspool of desire.

"I did knock. I got worried when you didn't answer," I lied.

"You didn't knock hard enough," he said, yawning as he pulled me on top of him.

I held my breath as I tried to ignore the sweetness of his breath. "If I was to hazard a guess, I'd say you needed me or maybe even longed for me."

"Don't get carried away," I smiled as I kissed him softly, finally giving in to temptation.

He brushed his tongue lightly against mine, teasing me.

God, he tasted delicious.

Every inch of my body trembled from the kiss. He made me want him badly.

The kiss intensified. So much so, that all common sense went flying out the window, and in its place was a crazed virgin in need of her first lover. Alex tugged at my sweater, pulling it over my head. I loosened my jeans, and together we slid them off, tossing them to the floor. I lay under him in my underwear as he looked down at me, assessing every inch of my body with his eyes flashing red.

I craved his touch and wanted his blood.

Biting hard into his wrist, the scent instantly burst inside my head and with no hesitation, I pulled his arm to me and drank. The warm blood gently slipped down my throat, its magnetism pulling me closer to him. I felt every wave of ecstasy coming through him. Sensing his need for me, I pushed his hand away, the blood still bursting inside me. I drew him down to me with force and his mouth explored my neck, kissing my throat, and gently gnawing on me. I wanted him so much, I thought I was going to explode.

He bit hard and it stung like hell, but soon enough, the pain was removed and replaced by something else. His thirst was insatiable, at first; his desire the driving force behind the bite. He slowed, gently supping my blood and abruptly coming to a halt before I reached a climax.

"If we don't stop, we're going to do something we'll both regret. It's not time."

I was breathless. "Oh my God, you can't make me feel like that and then stop!"

"It's not that I don't want to. Believe me, I do. We just can't. It would be wrong on so many levels," he said, shaking his head.

"So I shouldn't take this as rejection?" I said, feeling foolish.

"No way, Giselle. When it does happen it will be special, not just, you know, two horned up teens at it. I promise."

I felt humiliated. I was the one who had more or less instigated the whole thing and now it felt like the world's biggest anti-climax ever.

Rejection sucks.

"So, what happens now? I asked as I slipped my jeans on, shame written across my face.

"Well, you indulged in your third feed from me, so I guess a lot of things will happen now. I can almost bet the elders will be planning your consecration in the next few days, or even hours, and then we'll be married."

That certainly got my attention. "Married?" I choked on the word.

Laughing, he pulled me close to him. "Not like that, but similar. It's a lot less formal and a lot more fun than your usual mortal shindig. It'll be good. Wait and see, but first things first, I will go see Afanas and fill him in on the necessary things. The rest is our secret."

He winked at me. Grabbing me by the hand, he led me to the door. "I must make myself presentable and you might need to brush your hair," he mocked, twirling some of my hair between his fingers.

I left his room and walked silently, contemplating what almost happened back there. For someone who had strong beliefs about abstaining from sex, I gave losing my virginity a pretty good shot. My mother had brainwashed me from a young age that good girls just do not do that. They wait until they are in a long-term loving relationship, or marriage, the latter being mandatory.

Marriage? I was not ready for sex, let alone becoming a wife.

Chapter 7

The hot water flowed over me as I tried hard to wash away the past week. I wanted to get rid of any evidence of my erotic encounter with Alex and tried in vain to remove the dark shadow from within the hollow of my chest. I failed at both. I could still taste his blood and feel him on my skin. The blackness repelled the soap and remained there, its core embedded in my soul. A cluster of thoughts ran through my head, filling me with more grief and confusion.

"What's happening to me?" I whispered to myself.

It was one thing being brought into a world where everything was strange and new to me, but being told that I had to commit myself to Alex was another thing. I did not want to spend the rest of my life, or what was left of it, married to a complete stranger. The Alex I knew was no more, and, to be honest, I doubted I had ever known him. It had all been a lie, and one with a specific motive.

Yet something happened every time I was around him. It was almost as though I was being taken over by some force. Every bit of common sense told me that it was wrong and unnatural, yet I desired him and his blood. It was as if I had become spellbound. Nonetheless, all the thinking in the world was not about to change the fact that I was to become betrothed to him and, worse, I was to carry his child.

There had to be a way of escaping it all, but I did not know who to turn to, who I could trust. The worse part of it all was that I felt as though I had wished this all on myself, as though it was my own doing. If I was able to turn the clock back, I would not have called Alex. I would not have given Marc a reason to sleep with Evie, but, like always, everything is great in hindsight.

Somehow, everything I once knew was now gone. Giving in, I sat in the tub and cried. I mourned my lost youth, my freedom and, more importantly, I agonized over losing the right to choose my own path in life. Time passed as the water rested cold and still around my legs. My eyes were swollen from crying.

A faint knock at the door removed me from my inner torment and brought me to the present. I looked a mess, completely dishevelled. I refused to respond, remaining silent in the bath. I did not have the energy or confidence to talk to anyone. I wanted to be alone and allowed to wallow in my self-pity.

Persistence came with the next knock. A succession of loud bangs made me scramble to my feet, almost slipping in the now stagnant water. Pulling a robe over me, I answered the door, the noise pulsating through my head.

Standing before me was the same old woman I had bumped into in the corridor earlier. Her beady eye looked me up and down, whilst her lazy eye remained motionless. She mumbled something to me. As I was unable to understand, she raised her voice. Its pitch became a deafening sound.

Shaking my head, I shouted, "I'm sorry. I don't know what you're saying."

She continued to scold me in her strange language and pushed hard past me, shoving me up against the door. Her small frame was not as fragile as it looked.

I watched her move around the room, erratically looking for something. She talked constantly, repeating the same thing over and over. Her voice began to get on my nerves and I could feel my temper start to rise.

"Oh, shut up," I bellowed. "Just shut the hell up!"

Standing still, she eyed me and stared, long and hard. Her eyes were icy cold and red and they scared the crap out of me.

"Saty!" she pointed at me. "Saty! Diet'a ste neskoro."

Rushing past me, she went inside the wardrobe, throwing clothes to the floor. Suddenly, she roared with laughter. "Ano, to je jedna." She turned to me and handed me the dress.

"Saty!" Her smile was almost gentle.

"Dress? You want me to put the dress on?" I asked, holding the beautiful white gown in my hand.

"Ano, ano, saty!"

I did not understand a word she said, but I obviously had to wear the dress. Obediently, I did as I was told.

The dress was the most amazing thing I had ever seen. The fabric alone felt luxurious against my skin. The gown's chiffon bodice was completely covered with the most delicate jewelled beading and intricately embroidered pattern I had ever seen. A taffeta sash was placed high across the waist and was of a soft shade of grey marl. The skirt gracefully moved as I walked across the room. Standing in front of the mirror, I gasped. The dress was stunning on me. It made me feel like a princess.

"Krasny," the old woman smiled, holding her hand to her chest.

I did not have the heart to argue with her. So I stood still, staring at my reflection. That was when Atarah entered the room. Smiling, she walked up behind me and placed her hands on either side of my waist. Smelling of vanilla and rosewood, her scent wrapped itself around me, making me dizzy.

"You truly are beautiful, Giselle."

"Thanks," I falsely muttered.

Sighing, I turned to face her. I felt as though I could talk to her. She seemed so motherly and nurturing, and in an odd way, she reminded me of my mom, whom I missed dearly.

"Whatever is wrong?" She brushed the mess of hair from my face. "We will fix you up, but *bed* hair or not, you are the most stunning 'nevesta' I have seen in centuries."

"Nevesta?" I repeated, completely bemused.

"Bride! This is our mother tongue, Slovak."

I looked across to the old woman. "That's why I couldn't understand her. Who is she, anyway?"

Atarah, strolled over to the woman, and placing her arm around her she introduced us. "Giselle, this is Angelika. She is my mother and one of the elders. She takes it upon herself to take an active role in all rituals. She made the dress for you."

I was astonished at how different they were. I did not know if she meant Angelika was her birth mother or maker and now really was not the time for questions.

"Matka, to je Giselle, nas novy knazka."

"Ah, dcera, je hoden!" Angelika replied. Pure elation was written upon her face.

These breed of vampires deficd disbelief. In fact, they defied anything Hollywood ever tried to portray about the creatures of the night.

"Okay! I really don't know what you're saying. So, maybe we can talk a little English?" I felt embarrassed witnessing their bonding session. Or whatever it was.

"Oh, Giselle, I'm sorry. Mother doesn't speak English like us, so don't be alarmed by my conversing with her. She remains very true to her roots. Although we no longer live in Zemplin, we do like to hold on to some of our heritage."

I felt so small compared to Atarah and her mother. In fact, I was so different to them that I found it hard to believe I would be of any use to them. Then again, with all the trouble Angelika went to in order to make the dress, perhaps I was the most important commodity, after all.

Thinking so much gave me an unbelievable headache and I thought I was going to pass out. Taking a seat, I placed my head between my knees, taking long deep breaths. It didn't help.

"Giselle, take a sip of this. It will help." Atarah handed me a glass.

Taking it, I looked at her, wondering how someone who has killed to survive could be so loving to me. She treated me as though I was one of their own.

"What is it?

"Water," she laughed.

I drank and slowly regained my composure. God, it was hot in the room and the air that flowed in through the open window did not help.

The full moon shone bright. Its brilliance highlighted the crystal beading on the breast of my dress. The beads shimmered and danced with every flicker of the moonbeams.

Atarah, stood behind me and gently brushed my hair. She pulled it back and fixed some pins in place. Angelika rubbed some blusher onto my cheeks and applied some mascara and gloss. It was very basic, but when I saw my reflection, I was dumbfounded. I had been completely transformed from the girl who wore the most amazing dress ever, to a girl who deserved to wear anything she wanted. I was beautiful and felt beautiful, too.

Alarming as it might have been, I was quite excited. Sounds pretty crazy, but I think I got caught up in the moment, and being made a fuss of was definitely something I could get used to. But, as always, reality has a nasty way of hitting you hard in the face.

Walking behind Atarah and Angelika as they led me through corridors that looked like something out of a gothic fairy tale, I felt like a lamb being led to slaughter. The walls were a strange shade of pomegranate, its boldness illuminated by softly lit candles. The wooden floors were temporarily covered with a bluish-red runner that ran the whole length of the hall. Amaranthine drapes hung over the grand bay windows. The air had a distinct aroma, and although I could not quite place the smell I was sure it was incense. Its strong, fragrant smoke brushed the back of my nostrils, resulting in a few disapproving sneezes.

I sniffled, "Excuse me!" as we entered the hall through a large set of oak doors.

It was a very dramatic entrance. Standing below me were hundreds of unknown faces. A few stood out, but they were strangers all the same. They wore a mixture of black and purple clothes. The women were dressed in floor-length gowns, their hair pulled back tight and their hands covered by long lace gloves. The men's attire consisted of black herringbone frockcoats with matching black trousers. All wore purple shirts with black cravats.

I looked around, trying to find Alex and there he stood with Leonid in front of an altar. It was the most spectacular scene I had ever witnessed. Lighted candles and floral arrangements of violets, orchids, red roses, lilies, and irises filled the entire room. The scent was overwhelming.

Silence fell and all eyes were on me. My stomach churned and panic set in. I wanted to run through the doors and as far from there as I could, but behind me were two large men standing in front of the doors. They were not going to move for me.

I stood alone and watched the smile spread across Alex's face as he ushered me to him. I must have floated down the stairs, as I cannot remember walking down. The crowd moved as I walked down an aisle strewn with rose petals.

Alex looked amazing. I had never seen him look so handsome. He wore identical clothes to the rest of the men, except that his cravat matched the grey marl in the sash I wore around my waist. His smile illuminated the whole room and in normal circumstances, it would have melted my heart, but there was something sinister in his eyes. A deep redness flickered in the light of the candles.

I was so out of my depth. Taking my hand, he led me toward a stone slab in front of the altar.

Shaking, my voice quivered as I whispered to him. "What's going on?"

"It's your consecration. Remember, you will be blessed tonight. Just follow my lead."

He was so calm and it seemed that he expected me to mirror his demure behaviour. I was anything but calm. Sweat began to seep into the palms of my hands. So many eyes were upon me.

Breathe, Giselle. Just breathe!

Alex directed me to lie down upon the stone slab. I obliged and rested my body on the cold rock beneath me. Incense filled the space around me. There was no air, just smoky fumes. There were four men, one standing at each corner of the slab and each was holding a staff. Their eyes filled with the crimson tide that was visible in both Alex and Leonid. Alex stood back and disappeared behind his father. I was alone with the strange men, each mumbling to himself.

From the altar came the voice of someone I knew. Atarah.

"Tonight, we rejoice in the awakening of our sister, Giselle. She will be the vessel in which our new blood will run. It has been spoken by our forefathers that a mortal will bear the child of our beloved Prince Alexander. Our Goddess Lilith blesses this union and with her consent, we will commence."

Not a sound was heard. I lay still and held my own breath. Wind blew around the room, sending shivers down my spine. Each of the four men placed their right hand upon me. Joining them was Alex and his father, Leonid.

"You are a child of our Goddess Lilith and I ask her to bless you." Atarah's voice echoed through the room. I could feel the power that came with her words.

One of the men touched my head and spoke, "May your mind be blessed so that you can receive the wisdom of the Goddess."

Another touched my eyes. "May your eyes be blessed so that you can see clearly upon this path chosen for you."

My lips were next. "May your lips be blessed so that you will always speak with honour, respect, and love."

A hand was placed on my chest. "May your heart be blessed so that you may love and be loved throughout life's long path."

Alex placed his right hand on my abdomen. "May your womb be blessed so that you may respect the creation of life and thus be the giver of life." His smile was gentle.

Leonid was last. Standing at my feet he spoke, "May your feet be blessed so that you may walk alongside the Goddess and always place your trust in her."

I was helped to my feet by Alex. Atarah walked over to us, her face serious and full of passion.

"Tonight, you, Giselle, will pledge your commitment to the Goddess. You will walk with her beside you and ask her to guide you on this journey. Do you pledge to honour her and ask her that she allow you to walk alongside her?"

Alex nodded and I weakly whispered a small, "Yes."

"As you will, so it shall be."

The four candles were blown out and applause followed.

"Is it over?" I whispered in his ear.

"Almost done. There is just one more thing." He held my hand and we walked before the altar.

A man stood in front of us. He took my right hand and placed it in Alex's left.

"Welcome all. We are here this extraordinary night to celebrate the joining of Prince Alexander and Giselle. They ask for your blessing, encouragement, and lifelong support for their decision to become one. Giselle, do you come here of your own free will?"

I hesitated. I did not know what to make of this and felt awkward by lying. Deep inside, it was still a lie. "Yes."

"Alexander, do you come here of your own free will?"

"Yes."

"A ring is an unbroken circle, a symbol of harmony, of unending love, representative of this greater circle of life in which we all are spiritually connected. Giselle, do you carry with you this symbol of love?"

Atarah placed an engraved silver ring in my hand.

Another lie. "Yes, I do."

I kept thinking, *I have no choice. It is either this or something worse.*

"Please, place the ring on Alexander's left hand and repeat after me: You cannot possess me, for I belong to myself, but while we both wish it, I give to you that which is mine to give. You cannot control me, for I am a free person, but I shall serve you in those ways that you require and the nectar will taste sweeter from my hand. This is the vow I pledge to you. This is the union of equals."

I hesitated and faltered, stumbling on some of the words. The gravity of the situation caught within my throat and I felt the urge to scream and cry.

Alex repeated his vows and placed the ring on my left hand. Holding it tight, he refused to let go. I could not fight, although I thought about hitting him right across his face.

"Giselle and Alexander, tonight the moon stands witness to your union. You have made an eternal commitment to one another. You are bound by that commitment. You must honour each other for eternity. Having joined in this sacred union, I may now pronounce you husband and wife. Alexander and Giselle Baranski, you may kiss each other."

What a load of horseshit, I thought.

Alex interrupted my train of thought as he placed his hands at either side of my face and pulled me to his lips. His lips met mine. I tried resisting his mouth, but soon found myself falling for the same sweet aroma that poured from every crevice of his body.

It was irresistible. He was irresistible.

Hell. What had I gotten myself into?

'Hell' was the operative word.

Chapter 8

The next few hours before sunrise were a mixture of misery and confusion. I smiled pleasantly as I was wished well. Congratulations flowed out of every mouth and all the while, Atarah and Leonid sat back with smug grins on their faces. Well, on her face.

I felt like a fraud. I did not love Alex. I could not bring myself to think of him as anything other than a vampire. I did not see him the same way as I once did. He had forced me into an impossible situation and he was wholly responsible for my fate.

As dawn approached, weariness got the best of me. I wore it well upon my face, getting the attention of an unwanted admirer.

"Dearest Giselle, you made a beautiful bride, but I dare say the events have taken their toll on you."

His bluish black hair was a striking match for his blue eyes. He had caught me off guard and I forgot myself.

"Yeah. You could say I'm done in, but others might suggest otherwise."

"How do you mean?"

"Well, it is common knowledge that the wedding night follows the vows."

Laughing, he brushed his hand through his shiny black hair. "But one must comply with one's pledge."

"You don't say!" Mockingly, I laughed and it was obvious I amused him. "And you are?"

"How rude of me. I am Antoine Vilniv. It is a pleasure to meet you, Your Grace." His bow made me laugh. He was very different to many of the vampires there that night. He was not serious. He was funny. It definitely helped with the seriousness of my situation and had me at complete ease; kinda odd considering what had just taken place.

"Nice to meet you, too, Antoine."

"Now that the formalities are done with, tell me, how does it feel to be the one to snag his Lordship?" His sarcasm was a breath of fresh air.

"Put it like this, I'm a little afraid and so not ready for any of this bullshit. The deed has been done. Better to get on with it and hope for the best. I'm curious, though. What do you mean that I was 'the one to snag him'? If I am being honest, I always thought he was gay!" I lied.

Antoine laughed hard. Atarah looked over and her stern look said it all, condemnation. I felt my cheeks flush, but I broke the gaze to find Alex standing by my side.

"So, this is where all the fun is to be had?" he remarked as he slyly flashed his fangs.

"Cousin, your bride has a mammoth sense of humour. You must bring her to court more often." He kissed me on the cheek and took Alex by the hand. A firm handshake took place. "Congratulations. She is truly beautiful."

Alex nodded his agreement and placed his arm tightly around my waist, possessively. We passed the reducing crowd and bade our farewells to Atarah and Leonid.

I felt sick thinking about being alone with Alex. I did not trust myself and I did not want to lose control. Atarah pulled me off to the side. She clearly had something on her mind.

"I trust that your little encounter the other night didn't result in you losing too much of your virtue."

I began to defend myself, only to have her brush me off.

"If you feel nervous, you must follow a man's lead. He will teach you to be a lover. But to throw caution to the wind, it would be wise to remember that the whole purpose of the consummation is to become 'tehotna' – pregnant. Always remember your place, Giselle. Sleep well, child." She placed a kiss on my forehead.

Atarah's demeanour was beginning to change, and this frightened me almost as much as the thought of losing my virginity did.

"Goodnight, children." Leonid bowed and the two of them walked out of the hall, leaving me alone with Alex.

Sunrise was imminent and as Alex led me away from the hall I again felt sick. Once in 'our' room, nervousness crept in and I instantly feared the inevitable. I was completely vulnerable. He took me by the hands and directed me to the bed. I trembled as he embraced me in his arms. His strong torso almost crushed my head.

He held on to me for a few minutes before breaking away. Looking down at me, he pulled the pins from my hair, allowing it to fall loose around my shoulders. Not making a sound he walked behind me, unzipping the dress. It fell to the floor, leaving me standing there in my underwear and heels. He brushed his hand over my abdomen, sliding his fingers across the top of my panties. Gently kissing the back of my neck, he slowly opened his mouth, his fangs brushing against my skin. I shivered. I was shaking with anticipation, fear and excitement rolled into one.

Alex turned me around to face him, his eyes aglow. I could feel the pull of desire and, trying not to give in, I paced back from him, hitting the solid wall behind me.

Watching me, he stripped, throwing every piece of clothing furiously to the floor. Naked, he walked up to me pushing me hard against the wall, and bit hard into my neck. The pain was unbearable and I cried out. He drank hard from me, not letting go of my wrists.

Soon enough, the pain turned into something else. It spread deep from within, a fire bursting through me. I could feel him, every thought and feeling he had. I could sense his arousal and his anger. He wanted to teach me a lesson, but his longing and lust for me ruled his emotions. I easily gave in to the wanting.

He loosened his grip and immediately, I ran my fingers through his hair. God, I wanted him so badly. He broke away from my neck, his lips red. Licking them, I tasted my own blood and it stimulated every sense in my body.

We gazed at each other. Pulling me by my hands, he thrust me down onto the bed and moved directly over me, removing my underwear. His hands and mouth explored parts of me that had never been touched.

I never thought that being submissive would be a turn on, but, believe me, I had never desired anyone so much. At that moment I was his. I was the object of his desire.

Kissing him as his strong arms supported him, he eased himself into me. I tightened myself, almost afraid of the act itself. I stung and the burning sensation that intensified inside me began to simmer as something changed. The pain became something else. Light ripples of euphoria tingled its way throughout my body, leaving me breathless as I pulled him closer to me, our bodies moving in rhythm.

We were as one. All the anger I felt towards him melted and in its place, I found myself longing for him and his body. He made love to me as I had always imagined. It felt magical and with each movement, I craved him more. He brought me to the peak of ecstasy more than once. My body writhed uncontrollably each time.

Afterwards, I lay in his arms in silence and guilt welled up inside me. I longed for my mother. I wanted her to hold me and tell me all would be ok, but I knew deep in my heart that nothing could take away my addiction to Alex and I dreaded the future.

Sleep refused to come to me. I fought hard with my conscience. I tried to find some place in my mind to escape to, but nothing could save me.

I silently crept out from under Alex's embrace and put the dress on. Leaving the room brought a great sense of freedom, if only momentarily. I felt alive. I wanted one thing only, my mother.

Walking down the long corridor, I knew exactly where I was going and concentrated on getting to the one place in which I knew I would have a chance of getting in touch with my mother. Before entering the room, I looked around making sure no one saw me. I was pretty confident they would all be fast asleep.

The rain hit hard against the window of Afanas' study. The raging wind that accompanied it made the hairs on the back of my neck stand on edge. I went through the drawers in search of anything that gave me a chance of talking to my mother. As Alex had told me earlier in the week, I was permitted to call home weekly. Now was the perfect time to make contact.

Books, many of them in another language, some files with dates and times, and then there it was, a file with my name on it. Taking it out, I sat down on the floor and opened it up.

Every detail was accounted for: my date of birth, my parents, everything down to my favourite foods, dislikes, and Marc. Why did they need so much stuff on Marc? He was of little importance; just my one-time boyfriend, the love of my life.

A list of names stood out. Half the female faculty of my school, *De La Salle*, back home in Minneapolis, were listed. One name stood out a mile, Evie Stokes.

Christ.

I could not believe that Afanas had a file on me and I was even more shocked that Evie was listed amongst 'the desirable candidates.' *What was going on?*

Shocked, I did not hear Afanas as he entered the room. Once I realised I was not alone, I shoved the paperwork under the sofa and tried to look innocent. He was as surprised as me.

"Giselle!" He moved lightly across the floor. "What is it you require at this ungodly hour?"

I glanced at the clock. "It's only five p.m."

"In your old world, yes, it is early, but here, this is still the night. I'm sure you've noticed your daytime schedule has changed somewhat."

"Yeah, I guess a lot of things have changed. Why aren't you still asleep, then?" I asked as I got to my feet, trying not to draw attention to the file under the sofa.

"One has been restless, and as always, there is so much to be done." He sat behind his desk and eyed me. "What is it you want?"

"I . . . I was hoping to call my mother. I'm a little homesick and just, you know, wish she were here."

"Of course, you are home sick. It is natural for one to seek comfort in the arms of one's mother. After all, you are still human, so to speak."

"So, can I?"

"Yes, you may. Please take a seat."

I sat down and crossed my legs. Afanas looked through his drawers. He seemed confused. Agitated, he scratched the tip of his chin and looked at me.

"Strange. I swore I had left your contact details in here, but I'm sure I've only misplaced them. Do you by any chance know your own number?"

"Yeah." I snickered at him.

"You dial zero, zero, one, and then your own number . . ."

"Yeah, I know the rest. Thanks."

I picked up the receiver, dialed the number and waited nervously for someone to answer.

"Hello." My mother answered the phone sleepily. Her voice sounded the same as always, soft. God, I missed her so much.

"Mom, it's me."

"Giselle! Oh, honey. We've been so worried. Your poor father is beside himself with grief."

"I'm sorry. I really am. I just . . . I had to get away for a bit . . ." She cut me off.

"This is so typical of you. Why didn't you just tell us that you and Marc had some kind of falling out? We could have helped. I would have helped."

"Mom, not even you could fix it."

"Have you any idea what we have gone through these past nine days? Marc is absolutely distraught. The poor boy doesn't know what to do with himself. Whatever he has done, surely it is worth forgiving."

"Oh, Mom. You really have no idea, do you?"

She paused. "No, just that you two had a falling out at the prom. Or something like that. I don't listen to idle gossip," she lied.

"Mom, the gossip is true. Marc slept with Evie and recorded it. Someone thought it would be great to leave a copy of it in my locker. I have never been so humiliated," I cried, the tears falling over my hand as I held the phone to my ear.

"Don't cry, Sweetie."

"How can I not cry? I love him, or at least I did. I'm so sorry for putting you through this. I promise I'll make it up to both you and Daddy soon."

"You have nothing to be sorry for. I just wish you had told me before now. Maybe, I could have done something. Please come home, Giselle." Her voice broke.

She pleaded with me, but the look in Afanas's eyes told me to end the conversation.

"I can't, Mom. I just can't. I'm sorry. I'll call you soon. I love you." I cut her off before she could say any more and cried.

Afanas put his cold hands on mine. My tears fell uncontrollably over my reddened cheeks.

"Don't burden yourself with such grief. Things are better this way. I think it would best that you retire for the rest of the evening. It will do you some good."

I whispered, "Okay," as I sobbed, walking to the door.

Leaving the room, I walked in a daze down the hall. The cold air from the wind crept in through every gap and crevice in the vacant hall. It whistled eerily as I tried to control my emotions. I felt depressed and lacked the will to carry on. I wanted to end it all. Maybe death would help me escape this nightmare. Suicide could not be any worse than what I was going through.

A loud crash caught my attention. I spun round, realising one of the bay windows had opened. The curtains flew angrily over me as I stretched out to grab hold of the handle. Looking down, I considered how high I was. Just high enough to cause serious damage. Maybe even fatal damage.

Breathing heavily, I grabbed a hold on the windowsill, balancing myself as I placed my legs over the ledge. The wind violently blew my dress around my legs, its coldness meeting the warmth of my body and sending a series of shivers through me. Closing my eyes, I slowly let go of the windowsill and edged slightly forward.

"If you're serious, I can help you think of less painful ways to die." A voice came from behind me.

Antoine.

"But, I doubt that you are serious at all," he mocked.

"You don't know me. Okay! Don't you dare try and assume what I'm capable of."

"Then jump. I dare you."

The words echoed through my head and for a split second, I let go of the ledge and leaned forward. Gazing at the ground below, I seriously considered ending it all. As Wilde himself stated, 'The only way to get rid of temptation is to yield to it,' and boy, was I yielding.

I felt Antoine's hand slide around my waist. Aromas of roasted nuts, apples, and cocoa danced in my nose. I inhaled the infusion and let him pull me clear of the window ledge. Once I was in the safety of the hall he quickly let go. His dark blue eyes fixed on mine.

"What in hell's name were you thinking of?" He raised his voice, but not loud enough to attract unwanted attention.

I stood trembling. The realisation of what I had almost done hit me smack in the face. "I . . . I . . . I just can't take anymore of this. I'm just not strong enough."

"So you decide to climb out of a four storey window?"

"It seemed right at the time."

"How could you think killing yourself would solve anything?" There was genuine concern in his voice.

"I don't know what I'm thinking or feeling any more. I . . . I just wish I'd wake up and that this was all some bad dream."

"Giselle, I can't even compare myself with you, but I can offer you this, I think it takes a strong willed person to turn their fates around. I believe you are strong enough to overcome your fears and embrace your new life. After all, if you were to return to your 'normal life,' things would never be the same. You would have a hunger and nothing you'd consume would ever satisfy you. You must realise that!"

"I don't know, Antoine. I mean, I'm just some high school girl who believed in happy ever afters. My heart got broken and now this . . . I don't love him. I can't. Too much has happened, but he's got some kind of power over me. I lose control of all my senses and something takes over . . . and I hate it." I wept.

Crying in his arms felt like a weight had been lifted from my shoulders. Antoine was very different from Alex. He listened and offered advice. He knew all the right things to say. He seemed so real. He attentively brushed my hair as I sobbed into his chest. I held onto him tightly, afraid to let go, but I was also afraid temptation would latch on to my weaknesses. If it were not for the red glow of his eyes, I could not have felt more at home.

Chapter 9

Shocked by my sudden feelings towards Antoine, I pulled myself out of his arms. Awkwardness replaced the warmth of our embrace. I found myself clamming up, embarrassed by my feeble attempt at suicide. His deep blue eyes fixed their gaze on mine. Ignoring their lure, I made light of the encounter, trying desperately to focus on something other than him.

"I guess I better go. I'm pretty sure Alex will be worried. Thanks for not letting me fall to my death."

Smiling, his fangs glistened in the moonlight. "I would save you no matter how grim your fate was. And if I were Alexander, I'd be worried too. Good day, sweet Princess."

Bowing before me, he looked up at me. His eyes spoke a thousand words and at that moment my heart melted.

Wake up, girl! What are you thinking of?

I rushed back to the room, not once looking back to see Antoine watching me. I felt guilty. I knew I had not done anything wrong, but thinking about another while my 'new husband' slept was not the act of a 'good' wife. Trying to concentrate on the day/night ahead, I indulged myself in a hot soapy bath. I avoided looking at the darkness between my breasts and allowed my body to be submerged by the bubbles.

Heaven.

I felt his presence before he spoke. His scent was unique and I was now fully aware of his every move. Alex was now part of me. He was a permanent fixture in my life and there was no escape from it or from him.

"Is there room for one more?" he asked me.

"Sure, but it's getting kinda cold now." I tried not to sound disinterested. After all, we were meant to be in the throes of newly wedded passion. It did not bother him. He stepped out of his robe and climbed into the tub behind me.

As he pulled me back, I rested my head against his chest. His arms were strong and muscular and they wrapped themselves around me, holding me tightly and refusing to let go. His complexion was much paler than mine, but not a deathly white, more of a soft pearl. He was beautiful, too beautiful for me. I was nothing compared to him. I knew girls back home who were more curvaceous and drop dead gorgeous, girls more his type. I was just your normal girl next door. Nothing striking, except for the darkness that grew within.

"What is it that bothers you so much?" he asked.

"I'm okay. I'm just so tired . . . mentally."

"Oh, why?"

I laughed hysterically. "Oh my God, Alex. This is all so wrong."

He pushed me off him. I turned round to face him. "You didn't say that last night. I heard no complaints."

"Of course, you didn't. You did that thing . . . you make me lose control. I hate that you never give me a choice. I haven't had a say in any of this. If you love me, why use some weird vampire thing on me. Why not let me decide how far I want things to go?"

I got out of the tub and wrapped his robe around me. He followed behind me, shouting at me.

"Yeah, so what? I used a little compulsion on you. It's not exactly against my work ethic. Besides, you would never have given yourself to me willingly. You're still too hung up on that loser, Marc."

"Marc? What has he got to do with any of this? If I remember right, it was you who bit me and did some weird thing to my body, and now I'm married to you. This is all your doing. It has never been about love. It's been about you and your family's selfish needs. I am just the piggy in the middle. The glorified incubator for the bastard spawn of a vampire."

He hit me full smack across the face. I fell back and hit my head on the ground. Shocked, tears filled my eyes and, holding a hand to my cheek, I looked away from him. Trying to get up from the floor, I stumbled and fell back down. I gave in to the dizziness.

Holding in my cry, I watched him walk over to me. Naked and wet, he bent down in front of me. He brushed the cheek he had hit and I saw regret blaze across his face, but his words were cold.

"Do not ever talk to me like that again."

"I . . . I didn't mean anything."

"Yes. You. Did. You forget, I know you better than you know yourself. Remember, I have spent a long time waiting for you, but I am no fool and I will not have you, my wife, speak to me with such venom. Now, clean yourself up. We must feed."

Food was the last thing on my mind. I wanted to curl up into a ball and cry and sink into self pity. I was hurt that he had hit me and angry that I allowed him to get away with it. But I knew that I was not a match for him and never would be. For all I knew, if I were to ignore his requests then things would probably get a lot worse and I was not really in the mood to gamble.

I put on a pair of tight fitting jeans and a red cami top. Drying my hair, my stomach made some familiar noises and knew that food was probably a necessity. My thirst was hard to ignore and even in my emotional state, it was overwhelming.

As I walked alongside Alex, neither of us spoke. Obvious tension surrounded us and as we walked into a large marbled room. We met the gaze of both Atarah and Leonid. She sat demurely while gesturing to a small-framed girl who did not make eye contact with either of them. She retreated and walked over to us.

Her posture was bad and I was startled by how young she clearly was. She could not have been more than fifteen. Her golden hair was tied back in a tight bun. Her face was pretty, although dark circles sat under her ashen blue eyes and her lips were plump and red. She made no attempt to smile or frown. Her expression was blank and lifeless. I instantly felt sorry for her.

"Please, follow me, Your Majesties," she requested. Her voice was quiet and sad.

She led us to a small room that led off from where Atarah and Leonid sat sipping from crystal wine glasses. Walking inside, the sweet aroma was the first thing to hit my senses.

Blood.

A burst of excitement filled me. Looking around the room, I saw a skinny redheaded woman sitting back on a berry chaise lounge. A fire crackled in the background. Its heat made the air warm and increased the burning thirst in the back of my throat.

Alex took me by my hand and led me to her. She sat upright, a hunger in her own eyes. "Giselle, this is Natalia. She will be your donor tonight."

I was taken aback and shocked. I sat down beside her, nervously smiling. On the table beside her was a row of peculiar looking daggers. Each had a different symbol on its head, similar to the emblem that Afanas wore on his face. Unlike Alex, I did not have fangs and required a different method to obtain the blood.

Natalia reached over and picked the smallest dagger. Cutting deep into her inner thigh, I gasped in horror.

Opening her leg wide, she waited for me to move close to the wound. I felt disgusted that another woman wanted me near her, never mind to drink from her, but the scent of the sweet intoxicating fluid was too much to resist. Kneeling down, I slipped my tongue over the gash and instantly, the impulse of resistance left me.

The blood trickled downwards; its syrupy texture enticed my thirst. I gave in and found myself drinking the luxurious claret, letting it fill my mouth. Its velveteen texture exploded and satisfied the greed that consumed me. I pulled myself away from her. I looked deep into her eyes and she gasped. It was then that I had my first taste of a soul. It poured into me. The impact was like a thousand fireworks exploding inside me. Its fireball plunged within me and instantly I felt satisfied from the energy. I had never tasted anything so beautiful.

Shocked and bewildered, I stared at Natalia. She rested her head on the back of the lounger. Her eyes were sleepy and her face looked withdrawn. She was now a shadow of the person I had seen when I first came into the room.

Alex placed his hands on my shoulders, urging me to move. I walked to the side of the fireplace and stared at the flames dancing along the wooden logs. Alex took my place on the chaise lounge and proceeded to move his mouth over Natalia's neck. She let out a small cry. Before long, the cry turned into something else, pleasure. For a moment, a pang of jealousy came over me. Alex was my husband and seeing him feed from this stranger made my insides twist with anger. I could not help the feelings and surprised myself with the disgust that consumed me. I wanted to rip her throat out to make sure Alex would never be able to feed from her again. Uncomfortable, I cleared my throat.

Alex broke free from her neck and looked at me. His eyes were like fire. Blood dripped from his mouth. "What?" he snapped.

"Nothing," I replied timidly.

"Get. Out. Now!" he roared.

I anxiously moved to the door, not once looking back. I wanted to cry and I found it hard to understand the confusion of feelings flowing through me. One minute, I hated him. The next, I felt jealousy.

What was happening to me?

Walking out of the room without Alex by my side left me feeling empty. I hated the way Atarah stared at me. Her eyes said it all. She detested me for some reason and I was on a mission to find out why, or at least die trying. She was the one who encouraged me to follow Alex the night he first fed from me and I, unwittingly, was the fool.

She had made me think it was the right thing to do. I had followed all procedures up until now. I had obeyed every rule that had been thrown down my throat and for what? To be made to feel like some second-class citizen. I was not having any of it.

Walking briskly up to her, I scowled. Her face as beautiful as ever, but something was seriously off with her. She did not come across as the motherly figure I had first met. She was hardened and bitter. And I hated the cold.

Leonid was different. Ever since he had rescued me from the shadow creatures, he seemed to have warmed a little. I no longer felt threatened by him.

"So, what gives? Why am I being the one shunned and treated so badly?" I asked her, allowing Leonid to hear what I had to say.

"Excuse me?"

"You know exactly what I'm talking about!"

She laughed as she took another sip of what looked like red wine. "Oh, dearest Giselle, you are one for the dramatics. Really, don't burden yourself with nonsense. No one is treating you badly and not one person here wishes to shun you. Please, take a seat and have some refreshments."

Atarah looked up from her glass. She smiled at me. "Please, sit with us."

"I don't want to. I want to know why Alex won't leave Natalia," I asked, trying not to sound like a child or jealous spouse.

"Giselle, it has been a few weeks since Alexander, fed properly. I think he is allowed to indulge, do you not agree?"

The bitch. She was turning it all around.

"I agree that he should feed, but I don't agree with being kicked out. If he is my husband then shouldn't I have some say in how and who he drinks from?"

Leonid cleared his throat. Looking at me, he spoke softly, ignoring Atarah. "You are new to this. Given time, you will understand the primal urge to indulge your basic instincts. Right now, Alexander is feasting, consuming his source of her blood. There is no sexual chemistry, no desire behind his bite. Natalia, however, may experience moments of euphoria, but that is a consequence of Alexander's venom. She is merely food. It is nothing compared to what he experiences with you."

I could feel my cheeks blush. Embarrassed, I broke from his gaze and stared at the floor.

"Do you understand now?" Sarcasm flowed through her words. "Now, sit with us. Eat."

Sitting down beside them was an odd experience. Neither spoke. They just consumed the food from their plates. The table was laid with plenty of choices, croissants, jams, cold meats, trays full of cheeses, and fresh fruit. I sniggered.

"What do you find so amusing?" Leonid asked as I filled my plate.

"It's just . . . I didn't think vampires ate 'real' food."

He laughed loudly. "Our bodies need nutrients, just like yours. Remember, we live just like you, only minus our souls, and we enjoy the taste. Anything else you'd like to ask?"

"Yeah, why do I need the life source of my feeders?"

Silence fell among us. Atarah shuffled in her seat. Her long purple nails scraped irritatingly on the neck of her wine glass.

"Because, unlike us, you have the ability to drink the energy from the human psyche."

"Will it hurt them? Will they die? I don't want to hurt anyone."

"No. They will be drained and tired, but they will live."

"Why can't you do it? What's wrong with you?" I asked as I stuffed a huge slice of brie into my mouth.

"We were never in possession of a soul. The core of our essence has always been with the darkness. For those of us who inherited the gene, the soul left the body once they crossed over to the darkness. You are blessed with your soul and for one to consume that energy, their soul must still be intact."

"Oh! Wow, I never realised how complicated all of this is."

Alex walked out from the room looking radiant and calm. Watching him as he walked over to the table, he smiled at me. I remained inanimate. I was hurt because he had hit me and hurt because he had made me feel about two feet tall in front of Natalia.

"I trust you are satisfied?" Leonid asked Alex as he sat down beside me.

"Yes. I had almost forgotten how exquisite it can be direct from the source. To have no limitations."

I sat in silence, trying to swallow my mouthful of raspberries. I observed how the three of them interacted with each other. They seemed so awkward together. It was obvious that Alex and Leonid did not get along and I could feel the animosity between them.

Atarah favoured Alex over her husband. This again was apparent from her adoring looks that left me feeling very uncomfortable. My own relationship with my parents was not perfect, but it was not flawed like this. I had equal love for my mother and father and I longed for them. I wished to see them and feel their love. Not this mocking display of family life.

I missed home so much.

Alex ate a handful of blueberries, washed them down with a glass of grapefruit juice. His hands were model-like and I remembered how they had felt when he had touched me. I found it hard to believe that someone who portrayed so much gentleness and love could turn so nasty and use them as weapons.

Alex pulled me out of my train of thought and involved me in the conversation. "Was it better for you not to watch?" he asked me.

"Err . . . um, I, what?"

"Do you ever listen? It was better that you didn't see me feed from Natalia, don't you agree?"

"It all depends. You watched me, so why not show me the same courtesy? If nothing sordid was going on, why did you tell me to leave?"

"Because I did not want you to see me like that. Like the monster I am."

I was taken aback by his revelation. A pang of guilt built up inside my chest. I felt selfish for thinking about me, but his actions from earlier hung over us. He had caused us both pain. I could not imagine myself forgiving him.

Atarah and her smug grin left the table. She glided effortlessly across the room toward the door. Leonid followed, leaving us with something to ponder over. "What it lies in our power to do, it lies in our power not to do." He smiled at me and left.

"What does he mean?" I whispered.

"It could mean a thousand things."

"But it doesn't, does it?"

"No!"

"So?" Agitated, I pressed him for an answer. Anything.

"If we have the power to do something, we should do it in the right way. It must be good for everyone and ensure no harm comes to those we love, or at least that is what I believe it to mean."

"Oh, God. I think I get it."

I was not getting out of this any time soon and there was no way I could just run. Something inside told me I had to wait this out. I guess it was a situation that required me to go along with it, even if it meant succumbing to Alex's compulsion.

He got up and held his hand out to me. "Yes, I think you do and given time, you will learn to embrace this new life."

Chapter 10

The next two weeks passed in something of a haze, fueled by a mixture of blood and life energy. Being alone with Alex did not thrill me. He no longer scared me as he had before, and by giving myself to him willingly, I was able to have some control over my feelings. Yet, underneath his false displays of affection, I could sense something else, a small cluster of feelings that he held close. Every so often, I could feel them seep through into our moments of intimacy, often clouding my own judgment.

By closing my own heart to him, I refused to allow myself to fall victim to his own inner turmoil. Now I needed my faculties, but there was always the compulsion that got the better of me. I knew I had to try my best to overcome that controlling force, yet I had no way of really escaping the overwhelming sensation that came over me. In the end, it left me craving for more, like an addict wanting her next fix or drink.

Atarah had finally stepped back, or at least appeared to be giving us some much needed space and privacy. There were times when she seemed so warm and gentle, but on other occasions she scared the hell out of me. It was her eyes. They were so cold and full of hate, and when she looked at me, it was as though she resented having to share the room with me. Something about her relationship with Leonid appeared off, and when she caught me watching,(as she always did), she would stare at me until I mentally crumbled. She was more powerful than anyone I knew and I really did not want to get on the wrong side of her.

Afanas was becoming an ally, someone I could count on in my many moments of desperation. He would help me rationalize my feelings and helped un-cloud my judgments. He really was my only friend and although he still scared me, he was the only one who was honest with me. There was no sugar coating the harsh reality that I was expected to carry Alex's child. He was straight to the point and not once did he try to make it out to be something it was not.

Things were certainly moving fast and with Afanas's help, I was learning to control my thirst, something that seemed impossible at the beginning. I was also learning how to use the life energy to my advantage and one benefit was being able to disregard the imprint of darkness that had left its permanent mark between my breasts. Even though I could feel the presence of the darkness running through me, I was able to look at myself without hating what I saw.

"Will it always be there?" I asked Afanas.

Lifting his gaze from his journal, he placed the pen down and folded his arms. "The darkness is a part of you now and to answer your question, yes, it will always be there. Giselle, there is no changing what has been done. As you grow, so will the shadow. The stronger you become the stronger the hold darkness will have on you."

"Great, so not only do I suck at everything else, but now I will look like a freak forever."

"Oh, I can assure you that you are quite appealing to the eye. I doubt you understand just how special you are, but given time you will see things very differently."

Looking out of the window, he smiled and I could see the reflection of the moon clearly in his eyes. "The night is still young. Go and refresh your mind with a walk, or maybe indulge in something girls of your age like doing."

"Afanas, girls my age don't live like this, and they certainly wouldn't be caught dead sitting next to you," I joked.

"It has been quite some time since I had the blood of a young maiden." He closed his eyes and then looked at me slyly.

"Afanas, I was joking," I said, worried.

"And so was I." He smirked menacingly.

Before I left to the room, I walked over to him and placed a kiss on his cheek. It caught him off guard and for a moment, he did not react. Then came a small smile and sad eyes. "You truly are unique. Now go. I need peace and quiet."

Smiling, I left him to work on his journals and walked out into the night.

✦ ✦ ✦

The night air was hot and sticky. The weather was typical for the time of year and left me very restless. Although the night had become my day, I found it hard to focus. My dreams left me exhausted and I pined for a life far from here. I was not happy, but I was trying so hard to accept my new life. What else could I do? Everywhere I turned there were obstacles in my path. There was no escape.

Alex avoided talking about anything other than our imminent plans. It was as though our previous life back in Minneapolis had never existed and it was as though I was expected to forget about everything I loved.

The thought of me conceiving his child scared me beyond imagination. I was not ready for motherhood. I had not even graduated from high school and trying to talk sense into Alex was a complete waste of time. Our relationship was far from perfect and I was sure there were many secrets yet to be revealed.

The one thing that did linger in my thoughts was the file I had found in Afanas' study. Evie Stokes' name played over and over again in my mind – there was no escape from that bitch. Baffled by the significance of the file, I was eager to find out and willing to do just about anything, no matter the cost.

Alex walked into the garden. His presence was known to me before I could see him. I was in tune with his every move and my senses where becoming more astute every time I drank from him. He looked radiant and his eyes were calm and satisfied. He fed more frequently than me and although I was not happy about some of the feeders, I turned a blind eye. Remembering Leonid's explanation sobered any jealous rage inside.

I sat quietly at the fountain, watching the water flow as the moonlight danced between each trickle. I felt his hand slide across the back of my neck as he perched himself beside me. His hands were big and beautiful. I knew how gentle they felt against my naked skin, but I was also aware of how powerful they could be when used as a weapon.

"So, this is where you've been hiding," he said as he played with the loose hair that fell over my shoulders.

"I wouldn't say I've been hiding. Just taking a little 'me' time. Besides, it's a gorgeous night and what else is there to do?"

"Ah, 'me time'," he mocked. "We could always find something to do." He winked at me.

Playfully, I thumped him on the arm. Wincing, he pulled me into his arms, embracing me tight. I tried to fight back, arching my back away from him and felt his mouth search for my lips. The heat from his breath lit every fire within my body. Willpower was not my best attribute and within seconds I was kissing him forcefully. My tongue explored inside his mouth while his hands caressed the side of my thighs and we sank into our world of want and greed. He had won again.

A noise close by caught my attention. Something moved beyond the bush at the far wall and it paused while Alex and I looked. The solid brick wall stood over eight feet in height and towered over the boundaries of the estate. It was hard to imagine anything clearing it and soon my imagination, got the better of me.

"It's them again, isn't it?" I shook.

"Who?"

"Nothing. It's just my imagination," I lied.

"Tell me, Giselle. I can feel the lie." His voice became harsher.

"Them . . . The shadow creatures." My voice trembled at the mention of their name.

Alex looked at me, a puzzled expression swept over his face. "How do you know of them?"

It then dawned on me that Alex never knew about my little excursion down into the valley and my run in with the shadow creatures and my rescue by Leonid. Alex would be pissed.

"A few weeks back, I couldn't sleep and went for a walk . . . you know, past the boundaries. Only, I didn't know then that the walls were boundaries."

"You left the safety of estate? Do you know what could have happened to you?"

"I never knew . . . I didn't mean to cause trouble. I just needed to escape, you know. So much had happened. I only meant to go for a walk and come back. I didn't realise those things were watching me and when they attacked me . . ."

"They attacked you? That's impossible! If they had attacked, you would not be here. You would not have survived."

"But . . . He . . . he saved me."

"Who?"

"Leonid. Your father rescued me."

I knew that Alex would be angry, but I never expected him to explode. His eyes flashed amber red like the fires of hell blazing bright. Staring into my face, the fury I saw in his was like nothing I had ever seen before. It danced across his features. The Alex I thought I had known was gone.

His fangs were down, his nails dug deeply into my flesh and his delicious sweet scent had disappeared. In its place, I could smell deep burning sulphur, its suffocating odour hitting the back of my nose like a smoke bomb exploding.

"My father?" he spat into my face. "You allowed yourself to become the victim!"

Throwing me to the warm, dry ground, Alex disappeared into the night. Silence surrounded me as I became aware of my rapid heartbeat. I could sense the danger; it filled the night air around me. At that precise moment, I was alone and vulnerable.

Sitting on the warm, dry ground, I saw the yellow feral eyes staring at me through the canopy of the trees. Sitting still and lifeless, they watched me as I froze. My stomach knotted up once I realised there was not another soul outside with me and getting to my feet I retreated back to the house, closing the door firmly behind me.

The shouting was the first thing to grab hold of my attention. I followed the direction of the echoes, stopping outside Afanas' study.

Afanas growled. "You dare speak to me like that again and I can assure you . . ."

"Don't threaten me, old man. Remember your position here. Your opinion has never mattered. Why think it is of any importance now?" Alex ridiculed Afanas.

"Alexander, that is enough," Leonid bellowed. "Afanas is a much respected member of this lair. His viewpoint is the foundation of our beliefs. Have some respect. It is I with whom you have issues."

"Yes, you . . . Do you think it is right for my father to tend to my problems or my wife's? Did she ask for your help? No!"

"So I was supposed to allow them to take her?" Leonid sounded surprised.

"Yes, if that was the will of the Goddess."

"Lilith would not have allowed her death. The creatures have had a long suspicion that the prophecy was being fulfilled. Giselle has had no training. She does not understand the dangers of our world."

"Why keep it a secret? Why didn't either of you tell me?" Alex yelled at his father.

"There was no reason to speak of it. What good would have come from informing you? You would have reacted the same way, losing your head over a minor issue. What is done cannot be undone."

"Don't walk away from me when I am talking to you," Alex blared at Leonid as he walked towards the door.

"Alexander, believe me when I say this, if you ever try to manipulate or talk down to either Afanas or me again, you will be banished for a lifetime. I will cut short your very existence. Remember, it was I who gave you life and it is in my power to claim that life and your bride. You would do well to keep that in mind."

He left the room and walked straight into me. He stood like a giant over me. His monstrous physique was lean and well defined. His blond hair was cut short, allowing his stern expression to dominate his face. He was beautiful. His bluish-grey eyes were large and round, and in the dim light of the hall, they simmered. The anger that had consumed them slowly evaporated, leaving them vulnerable, like glass. They lingered on mine, watching each expression on my face. I became flustered and blushed, the red burning bright on my cheeks.

"I'm . . . Sorry, um . . . Have you seen Alex?" I whimpered like a child of four.

"Don't pretend you didn't hear any of that. Alexander needs some time alone to reflect. Come, walk with me. There is someone I'd like you to meet." He directed me away from the door and like an obedient animal, I followed.

We walked east of the main building, heading towards an old stone structure. The tall willows partially enveloped its roof, as if they were shielding it from the world outside. Soft light flickered from the windows and as we entered, I was shocked by the presence of a frail old man seated in a large chair. His hair was silver with flecks of black streaked through the roots to the ends and it hung long and tidy over his shoulders.

Leonid walked over and bent down. He kissed the ring on the old man's left hand. The man recited something in Slovak. Leonid returned to his feet and called me over to him.

"Giselle, this is Vadim, our Prophet."

I stood in silence.

Vadim called me forward. His voice was like a thousand knives cutting through the wind as he spoke. "Do not let this pleasant exterior fool you, child. I am, after all, a killer. I am what I am, never forget that. But it was you who visited my dreams and brought hope to our troubled times. You are the key."

He held my gaze and then he began to recite some strange poem. "She will walk forth from darkness into light. At the moment of birth into the world, the child we seek, in the name of truth, will lead, and so shall become the first and be the last."

The words echoed in my head. Was I to conceive a child who would be some kind of leader and eventually die? Confused and tired, I sat down close to Vadim. He smelt different from Leonid and Alex.

His scent was sickeningly sweet. Intoxicating aromas of aged merlot and silky smooth blends of milk and honey sprung from him, making me dizzy. I twitched my nose in disapproval.

Leonid stood close by, his demeanour calm and relaxed. I had never seen him like this and I could not help but watch him as he drank wine from a silver lined glass.

Vadim spoke as I eyeballed Leonid. "I trust that you have consummated the union."

Oh my God! Embarrassed, I blushed. I could feel the heat rising from the back of my neck, hitting my cheeks like a train at a hundred miles an hour. "Well, yeah!" I replied.

I was not expecting questions about my sex life. I was uncomfortable, and relieved when Leonid interrupted.

"I can assure you, both Alexander and Giselle are following the agreement of their union."

"Very well. I trust that you will keep me informed of any developments."

Leonid nodded. "Giselle, it is time we left. After all, dawn will be upon us and I'm sure Alexander will be curious as to your whereabouts."

I got up and proceeded to follow Leonid. Turning back, I looked at Vadim. "My one request is that if I do have this child, I want to be his or her mother, not just someone who gave birth. That is my right."

He smiled. "But of course. I would not trust anyone else to raise the child."

We left and walked silently back towards the house. Leonid was clearly deep in thought when I spoke. "Leonid, can I ask you something?"

"Yes?" he replied, slowing his pace.

"Why did you save me from the shadow creatures?"

He stopped and looked at me, his dark eyes like a pool of juniper berries waiting for me to dive in. "Because I could not stand to see you come to any harm. Alexander is a fool if he cannot see how beautiful and special you are."

His words came as a shock to me.

"Oh!" I could sense his awkwardness. "I guess I'm glad you did. I kinda owe you my life."

With his back to me, his voice was barely audible. "You owe me nothing."

He continued to walk and I followed. Nothing more was said between us. Confused, I retreated to my room.

Alex was already in bed. The sun was beginning to rise, and its golden light crept in through the black, thickly lined drapes that covered the two bay windows. I slipped out of my clothes and crept in beside him. He did not acknowledge me and I watched him as he slept. I found myself soon drifting off to dreams of familiar settings and in the arms of another.

Marc.

Chapter 11

Marc ran after me, pointing the paintball gun at me. I squealed like a child as he got closer. I found overgrowth in the trees in front of me and crept down, silently holding my breath. I could hear his footsteps and twigs cracked as he moved closer.

"Come out, come out wherever you are!" he sang in a dorky voice.

Excitement built up inside me as I got ready to jump him and end this game, once and for all. I slowly made my way out from under the branches, aiming the gun at the back of his head. He was standing looking in the opposite direction. My finger rested on the trigger. Calmly I got ready, aimed, and fired.

Bang.

The red splatter of paint hit him right in the back of his left arm. He swung round, shocked. A broad smile spread across his face as he ran towards me.

"How'd you do that?" he laughed as he pulled me close to him.

"Ah, now that would be telling." I pulled the mask off my face. Pulling me close to him, Marc planted a kiss on my forehead.

"I love you!" he smoldered into my ear.

"I love you more," I teased. "Come on, let's go find the others." I held his hand as we made our way back to base camp.

Greg, Aaron, Cassie, and Mandy were already there. The girls laughed fiercely as Greg played out one of his usual shower room pranks. Mandy was Greg's girlfriend, and had been for a solid two months. It was pretty obvious from their 'pda's' that they were 'doing it,' and when I say 'doing it,' I mean third base was no longer on the agenda. It was the whole shebang.

Aaron saw us first and roared, "What took you so long? We were going to send out a search party or something." He laughed as he farted, holding a lighter at his ass. The flame shot out and Cassie squealed.

"I am so not sharing a tent with you tonight, Bozo."

"Awe, Babe, I was only getting rid of it. Better out than in. You know you want me!" Aaron groveled and he playfully nibbled on her stomach.

"I don't know about wanting you, but maybe you can make it up to me." She laughed and a hint of mischief blazed through her eyes.

"I pity you if you have to smell that all night long," Marc said as he sat down, pulling open a can of Budweiser. He gulped it down in one, letting out a belch as he threw the can over his shoulder.

"Pig!" I muttered.

He laughed and handed me one. "Nah, not my thing tonight!" I rejected the drink and happily sat back, watching everyone laugh and joke.

I was content and happy and loved every inch of my life.

* * *

Alex woke me from my dream. Sleepily, I sat up, rubbing my eyes. He sat opposite me, wearing blue flannel boxers. I observed his face as he battled with some kind of inner turmoil. I did not like when awkwardness controlled us. I much preferred our usual, nonchalantly way of doing things.

"What's wrong?" I asked.

He cleared his throat. "I'm sorry for the way I reacted earlier."

"It's okay," I said, uneasy.

"No, it's not. I behaved like a spoiled brat. I don't know what comes over me. Sometimes, I just feel like my father sticks his nose in everything I do. I mean, I can't even have you without him knowing every sordid little detail."

"What do you mean?" I asked.

He certainly had my attention now.

"I had to prove to them that I had taken your virginity."

"How?" I asked as I sat forward on the bed, my heart racing a hundred miles an hour.

He was clearly uneasy, which made my stomach turn. "By showing them the blood-stained sheet."

I shot out of the bed like a bullet. In front of the window, I paced, holding my hands to my head, trying to comprehend what he was saying. I could feel the sweat begin to gather on my brow and felt queasy.

"I'm so sorry. I know it sounds sick and twisted, but they just needed proof that you were no longer a virgin."

"Oh my God... Do they know everything about our sex life?" I cried.

"Yes, to a degree."

He tried to put his arms around me but I pushed him away. I rejected him. "How could you? I thought it was a union between two people, not me and your whole frigging family!"

"Giselle, come on. It's not like that and you know it."

"No! Don't even try, okay. Just leave me the hell alone. Get out. Get out now. God, I feel sick," I cried as I pushed him towards the door. "Get out and don't bother coming back here any time soon. I. Hate. You!"

Slamming the door behind him, I collapsed to the floor and cried. Feeling sick to the core, I crumbled inside. I could never forgive them for this. It was like I had been raped by both Alex and his family.

I hated them.

Like everything else that was happening in my life, I felt like I had suffered one blow too many. I could not take much more devastation and humiliation. Alex had crossed a line. Yeah, I know that not much of our relationship was based on any strong foundation, but I had thought we had made some kind of progress. This . . . this was sick beyond anything he had done to me. I felt powerless and trapped in a world that showed me no mercy.

Broken, I sat with my head against the door. Warm tears flowed down my cheeks like rain on a summer's day. Outside, I could hear the distant songs of birds in their full morning glory. I longed for my old life. I ached for the sun to wrap its arms around me and warm the broken heart inside.

Caught up within my thoughts, I did not notice the increasing vapour that began to fill the room. Its stagnant smell left me dizzy, disoriented. Before me, a white bearded man began to materialize. In his right hand, he held a staff and he was dressed in white. His eyes were grey and his face was a mass of wrinkles. He moved slowly towards me, his expression unreadable.

Calmly, I rose to my feet and trying not to lose my balance, I held onto the handle of the door. Warm air encased me as its heavenly heat ran through me, infusing every cell in my body. I felt at ease and fearless.

"Do not be frightened, child," he reassured me. "I am Bylun, and I have come to help you. You are in grave danger and must leave at once. Come, we do not have much time. Their lies will be your downfall."

Bylun ushered me towards him, and in a flash we were gone from the room. I felt queasy as I opened my eyes and stared around the large blue paneled room. Its high ceiling was painted in gold and sharp interlocking spirals shaded in sapphire spread from one end of the room to the other. The sheer dominance of it made me dizzy and I found myself grabbing a hold of Bylun's arm, taking him by surprise. Smiling at me, he took hold of my hand and together, we walked further into the room. Dim light shone in through the window, but I was not sure if it was day or night.

In the centre of the room, the silhouette of a man was sitting on what appeared to be a throne. It was large and its back was oval-shaped with armrests and had winged creatures intricately carved into it. Its golden brilliance dominated the room. It was its centrepiece, a place of power.

The closer I came, the more I recognized the man sitting in the chair. He smiled at me. His familiar blue eyes looked at me intently as I stood before him. The last time I was this close to him, he had dared me to jump to my death. In some ways, he saved me then, just as he had done now.

Antoine.

"How is this even possible?" I asked him.

"Many things are possible, sweet Giselle!" His voice was mesmerizing.

"I don't understand what's going on? Why did Bylun take me from my room?" I asked, my voice breaking. "I don't know how much more of this I can take." Tears welled in my eyes.

"Shush, waste no more tears," Antoine said as he wiped the tears that finally escaped. "There is so much you need to know and unfortunately, time is not on our side. Bylun here is a good friend and a strong ally. He is, of course, a white God, someone that the underworld rarely associates with. But, on rare occasions, like now, those of us who remain loyal to the throne seek the assistance of the Gods."

"I'm sorry, but . . . why?"

"Giselle, your body will be used as a vessel, a way for the hands of fate to change its course. If you are to bear the child of Alexander Baranski, you will have given birth to the start of an uprising, a war that will be more powerful than those fought by man. Your child would be the sole inheritor of darkness, thus resulting in your imminent death and of course, the death of Leonid." Bylun's strong voice echoed in my ear.

"My death . . . What's Leonid got to do with any of this?"

Antoine grabbed a hold of my shoulders and looked me in the eye. "Leonid has been taken for a fool. Vadim cannot be trusted. He did envisage you, but not the way you have been led to believe. You will be helping them embrace the darkness, Giselle. Alexander and Atarah are not what they seem. Between the three of them, they are on course to destroy those of us who believe human life to be sacred. They seek the ways of the old."

"But . . . Alex wouldn't do this to me."

"No, Giselle. He is devoted to Atarah. They have long since planned the uprising and you, my sweet Princess, have been nothing but a pawn in a very cruel game. He cares not for you. It is the Nelapsi who he seeks favour from. He is not to be trusted."

"How could you say that? You don't know us. You have no idea how he has been trying. I know he is slightly temperamental, but he has tried so hard to make me fit in. It makes me sick that you would even suggest that he and Atarah . . . God!" I roared.

"We do not lie. We speak only the truth and right now, it's your safety that is our concern. We have, what is it you say? Ah, we have opened up a whole can of worms." Antoine laughed as he loosened his grip on me and escorted me to a door that led from the back of the room and down a spiral staircase.

"Where are you taking me?"

"Some place where they can't sense you."

"Where? Because it seems that they can find me pretty much anywhere." My persistence was starting to pay off.

"Home, Giselle. You are to return home."

Home.

Just hearing that word sent a shiver down my spine, like a bolt of lightning striking me down. I was both excited and scared. I was apprehensive about returning to the place where I was born, but also of having to finally deal with the aftermath of the prom. I could not help but think about everything that had happened. I had so many questions and I felt like a fool for not having seen the connection between Alex and Atarah. I wore the stress of it all on my face and it obviously caught Antoine's attention.

"Don't worry. I will not leave your side. Well, not until you have returned home safely. I have already set up your protection. Between Bylun, me, and few others, you will be secure."

"But how? Alex will know where to find me. He will not give up so easily," I responded.

"Yes, but he is unaware of my involvement." Antoine was confident.

"Then how is this going to happen? So I just to place my life in your hands and act normal – like that could ever happen again. I mean, how can I face everyone back home? I can't even look at myself in the mirror anymore," I cried.

"Giselle, you are stronger than you believe. I promise you that from this moment forth I will not let you come to any kind of harm. Can you trust me?"

I wanted to believe him, to place all my trust in him. But after being betrayed by so many people in such a short period of time, I was reluctant to give my trust so willingly.

Bylun stood by my side. His gentle approach calmed me. "I would place my life in Antoine's hands, although I do not agree with his lifestyle. I do, however, believe that he has the goodness to prevail against all darkness and the power he possesses is one not to be trifled with."

"Very true, although I do have your one hundred percent backing," Antoine agreed, adding humour to an otherwise nightmarish situation.

"Okay, so let me get this straight. I can go home, return to my 'normal' life, do all the things I was meant to do in the first place and basically forget that Alex ever existed?"

Antoine and Bylun looked at each other. Again, their expressions were unreadable.

It was Antoine who broke the silence. "Yes, all things considered, you can try to live a normal life, but unfortunately, the past always has a way of catching up with you."

"Meaning what, exactly?"

"Giselle, Alexander will come for you. There is no doubt about that, but for now, you will be safe back in Minnesota. Remember, it is only a temporary solution. It will give us enough time to gather other nobles and make plans to bring Atarah and her minions down."

"But what about Leonid? We can't just leave him there, can we?"

"Leonid will be fine and I can bet my life that he will see through their schemes. Besides, I have made arrangements to meet with him once I have returned." His eyes were so calming. I was pretty sure he was using a little compulsion to calm me.

He took a hold of my hand and kissed it gently. His blue eyes looked up at mine and for the first time in a long while,

I felt my heart skip a beat. "Now, the long journey must begin. Sleep well, young princess."

Light-headed and dizzy, I stumbled and could hear my own heart beat slower. Its thump echoed in my head and my eyes began to lose focus. In a flash, I was out cold; again.

Chapter 12

It felt like only moments had passed since I fell asleep. I had no concept of how much time had passed and I was shocked to see that the sun was starting to break through the clouds that had accumulated in the night. The welcome sight of elm and evergreens made me feel welcomed and suddenly, I realised I was in Kenwood.

I was home.

A burst of excitement ran through me like a million stars exploding. Eager, I sat up straight in the back of the blacked out car as we drove closer to my house. Looking out of the window, I devoured every path, house, and car that we passed. I refused to take any of this for granted and wanted to imprint the memory of 'home' in my brain, refusing to ever forget where I came from.

The car slowly came to a stop. Antoine, who sat beside me, took hold of my hand and placed a necklace in my palm. Looking at it, I realised I had seen the same artwork in his throne. It was white gold with a miniature crown charm. Tiny writing was engraved on it, obviously in Slavic, a language I would never understand.

"Thank you, but I can't accept this," I spoke softly.

"It is merely a gift from me to you, but it also has some significance with your safety. See this writing? It's an old spell, binding you from harm."

"Oh. What does it say?" I was intrigued.

"This bit here . . ." He pointed to the back of the crown. "It says, 'In the shadows, evils hide, willing to take me from love's side, but with your help I shall be strong and exile what does me wrong. Send them away. Send them astray, never again to pass my way. So mote it be.' And this part says, 'In the Goddess's name, Lilith, we command thee'."

He placed it around my neck and secured it in place. Before I could say anything, my door was opened by a large, bald man who wore thick-rimmed sunglasses. On his face was the same emblem that Afanas wore. I could not see his eyes, but I was pretty sure they were deep red.

"Thank you," I said as I got out of the car.

My legs were like jelly and butterflies of excitement and anticipation built up inside me. I could not wait to have my mother wrap her arms around me, but I was so afraid of my father. I worried about how he would react when he saw me. Taking a deep breath, I stepped onto my drive. Pausing, I looked at Antoine. He smiled at me. A beautiful, caring expression spread across his face and it made me feel completely at ease.

"I'll be in touch. Stay safe, sweet Princess."

I had no time to say anything. The car drove off, leaving me alone looking at the house in front of me. My home was a traditional house, set on a hill overlooking the Lake of the Isles. Deep among the trees, it was a haven away from all the hassle of school life, a place where my heart truly belonged.

My mother's silver Sedan was in the drive. I walked around it as I slowly made my way to the front door. My heart skipped a beat as I bent down and found the spare key lying under a pot full of posies and geraniums, their strong, earthy, herbaceous scent soothed me, balancing my thoughts and giving me a spring in my step.

Turning the key, I entered the front hall. I was greeted by the same pictures of my youth; familiar surroundings that welcomed me home with open arms. I roamed from room to room, taking in every little detail, from the miniature fairies I had collected as a child to the more dramatic ornaments that were priceless collectables – my mother's pride.

Glancing at the clock, I realised that my parents would be close to getting out of bed. I had no clue what I was going to say and tried in vain to make things up inside my head, planning answers for each question, but came up with nothing. I was a useless liar and totally uncreative. I was just going to have to go along with whatever was coming my way.

No one was more surprised by my presence than my father when he walked into the kitchen. I sat by the centre isle with a cup of coffee in my hand. I meekly smiled as he dropped his morning papers, pure shock shooting across his face.

"Marilyn, I think you better come and see this," he shouted from where he stood.

From the hall, I heard my mother complain, "Oh, what is it now, Geoff?" She walked into my father, her eyes fixed on me. "Giselle!"

"Hi, Mom," I said, swallowing hard. "I thought it was time to come home."

My mother rushed up to me, grabbed me in her arms and held me tight. I could feel her sobs as she tried hard not to let go. My father stood back, observing us, a stern look on his face. He was going to be the one to administer the discipline. I could see it coming.

"Enough," he shouted. "Enough of this nonsense. Giselle, do you have any idea what you have put us through? We had just about accepted that you had left for good. And now you turn up unannounced and expect a welcome committee? You are in so much trouble, young lady."

"Daddy, I'm so sorry. I wasn't thinking straight," I cried.

"Not good enough. You are grounded for as long as I see fit. I don't want to hear excuses. In fact, anything you have to say will fall on deaf ears." He looked at me with hurt written upon his face.

"Daddy . . ." I tried again.

"You are excused." He picked up his papers and continued his journey to the breakfast room. No more was said and I did as I was told, retreating to my room.

I was exhausted and welcomed the sight of my neatly made bed. Nothing had been touched, except for the laundry that had been put away. Collapsing on the bed, I slept soundly until a loud knock awoke me from my dreams. Wearily, I tried to open my eyes. I rubbed at them, encouraging them to open and slowly, I realised that it was not a dream. I was really home in my own bed and hearing the familiar noises that would normally piss me off, my brothers arguing.

Before I reached the door, my sixteen-year-old brother, Ryan, burst into the room, throwing himself on my bed. He was followed by Kevin, my irritating thirteen-year-old baby brother.

"Heard you were home," Ryan said casually as he flicked through some outdated magazine he found on my side locker. "You know what they're all saying?" he added smugly.

"What?" I stubbornly asked.

"That you were knocked up and went AWOL to get rid of it." He laughed.

"Yeah, well you heard wrong, dumbass," I angrily retorted.

"Glad you're home, Sis," Kevin said. "It's been weird around here. Mom has been crazy. I swear I can't take her picking me up from soccer practice any more. She's out to ruin my life."

Getting out of the bed, I pulled on a sweatshirt and moved over to Kevin who was a miniature version of our father, tall and skinny with thick black hair.

"Glad to be back," I said as I threw my arms around him and gave him a kiss.

"Gross," he said as he left the room, red faced and wiping the side of his face.

"So, what gives?" Ryan asked.

"Nothing," I told him as I sat back down on the bed.

"Liar! I know what that jerk did. Of course, you made yourself look like a complete loser by running off like that."

"Really? So, what should I have done?" I asked him, folding my arms in protest.

"Come on, G, we all know you have a pretty mean right hook. Why not just kick her ass?"

I jumped off the bed again. This time I stood by the window and stared out across the lake, focusing my eyes on the trees in the distance. "Because, Ryan, I had my heart broken. I wasn't thinking straight. Running away seemed like the right thing at the time. I guess regret is something I'll have to learn to live with." I turned around to face him.

"You should have gotten Mom involved. She would have crucified him."

Ryan watched me as I paced back and forth. My hair was dishevelled as was my choice of bed wear, my favourite rocky horror show t-shirt and tiger pants.

"You've changed," he blurted out as I sat down beside him. He was serious and his deep brown eyes showed he cared.

"I guess I have. Sometimes, things happen and alter who we are," I said, sighing.

"Yeah, but don't you think it's time to . . . I don't know . . . move on? Forget Marc and Evie ever existed and just, you know, get laid by one of his friends?" He smiled.

"Eww. Oh yeah, I can see that solving all my problems. How's dad been? He won't even talk to me." I changed the subject.

"Dad is Dad. He'll cope. It's just . . . you broke his heart. You left and, well, he had to pick up the pieces. Kinda hard for a man who spends all his spare time tearing things apart. He'll come around. He always does. Mom, on the other hand, has gone all Stepford on us. We can't do anything or go anywhere without her panicking that we'll disappear as well. By the way, thanks for that. I was this close to getting it on with Brigitte Spencer."

"I'm sorry, Ryan. I didn't think about you or Kevin, but believe me, I'm not going away ever again. I'm home for good. Scouts honour." I held my right hand up in the air, knowing I was probably lying. "But seriously, Brigitte Spencer?" Both of us laughed out loud.

My mother knocked on the open door. "Honey, someone is here to see you," she said as she moved out of his way and he walked into my room. A face more familiar than anyone I ever knew. I had loved that face and had grown up looking into those beautiful eyes. He was to be my always and forever.

My mother called Ryan out into the hall and he closed the door behind him, giving me a look I knew only too well and mouthed a few words at me, "Sock it to him."

He stood in front of me. I wanted to ignore him, to pretend he was not there, but my gut instinct refused. I gave in and asked the simplest question of all.

"Why, Marc?"

Marc stood in silence with his hands in his pockets. He looked as miserable as I did and for a moment, I sympathized with him. He made no attempt to answer me. The only noise that I could hear was the pounding heartbeat that reverberated in my head. He looked tired and was a shadow of his former self.

Impatience got the best of me. Pent up anger flew from me in a violent rage as I slapped him hard across the face. He did not fight back, infuriating me even more. I slapped him again, but as I did, tears fell down my cheeks. My anger was winning and I could do nothing except continue to hit him until I ran out of breath and the urge to fight. Standing in front of him, I cried.

"Why Evie? Why her? Was I that bad of a girlfriend?" I sobbed.

He shook his head while his own tears fell as he broke his silence. His face was reddened, but it was his eyes that were full of tears and sorrow. "I can't excuse what I've done. I make myself sick just thinking about it."

"Marc, you screwed another girl behind my back! You promised you would wait for me and now it's too late."

"Please, Giselle. Please, give me another chance," he begged.

"I can't. I could never trust you again. You allowed it to happen. Live with it," I hissed coldly at him.

With more fight than I expected, he raised his voice, "Maybe you ought to ask your buddy about that night. After all, he was the one who set the whole damned thing up. I was the fool who fell for his scheme. He's always wanted you and I was constantly in his way."

"What? Who do you mean?"

"Oh, come on, G, your good, old buddy Alex. He was behind it all. I was too damned drunk and high to realise what was happening until, well, it was too late."

"What?"

"Alex threw a party at his place downtown. The pot was free, so me and a couple of the guys thought why not. Got stoned out of our minds and drank his bar dry. Next thing, Evie is all over me and Alex was cheering her on, saying it wouldn't leave the room. What happened there, stayed there. I had no idea that the whole thing had been a set up. I know I screwed up big time, but Jesus, Giselle, I deserve a little something here. I've beat myself up over this for months now. You can't punish me any more than I've already punished myself. I love you. It has always been you, only you."

I could hardly believe it. Was it all really true?

It all started to make sense now. The realisation of the past seven weeks came crashing home. Everything started to add up. Alex had been behind everything. He had coaxed Marc into having sex with Evie. The file I had found in Afanas' study had a list of girls – girls who would be easy prey; easy enough to sleep with Marc. The whole thing had been orchestrated by Alex as a way to make me defenceless.

It worked.

I had been in the dark, but now my eyes had been opened. Now, I would do anything to pay him back for the pain and torment he had caused me. He had clouded my thoughts long enough and now it was time to wake up and take action.

Marc and I looked at each other. We had shared so many firsts together and the one thing that was important had been taken from us both. There was nothing we could do to replace that lost innocence, but if we tried, then maybe our relationship could find some salvation.

I secretly hoped.

Marc walked up close to me. The familiar smell of his cologne floated around me. He was delicious and I wanted him to touch me. I wanted to feel his warm skin against mine.

Have him hold me, love me, and maybe, in time, we could share something more than this. At that moment, I had already forgiven him. I think he could sense that, because what happened next was the single most beautiful moment of my life. He gently pressed his lips against mine and kissed me. His sweet breath flew into me. I held onto him, refusing to let him go. I did not want to lose him again. I could have stayed in that brief embrace forever.

I really was home.

We never noticed my mother standing at the door. She cleared her throat, gaining our attention. She looked thinner than usual, but I put that down to the stress of my leaving. She smiled at us, her obvious approval written all over her face.

"Giselle, honey, I hate to interrupt, but you have another visitor, a man. He said he met you while you were on your travels," my mother said with a hint of irony in her voice.

"Oh, okay, um, I'll be down in a minute. I . . . need to change."

"Okay, Sweetie. I'll tell him you won't be long. Come along, Marc. Giselle needs her privacy."

They left the room, closing the door behind them. I rummaged through my wardrobe and chose a pair of denim shorts and my favourite Sponge Bob t-shirt. I brushed my hair into a loose ponytail and made no effort at putting on make-up. What was the point?

I shifted down the stairs at record speed, coming to a halt when I saw the neatly dressed man sitting in our living room, drinking tea from one of my mother's finest cups and saucers.

Leonid.

I placed my hand over the charm and prayed for protection, even if I did not believe.

Goddess, be by my side.

He smiled at me. His eyes were an odd shade of green, but I stayed my distance and reluctantly replied when he spoke to me.

"Giselle, you never told me how enchanting your mother is," he mused.

My poor mother loved the praise. She smiled and gushed, "Oh, Mr. Baranski, it is nothing really."

"Yeah, my mother kinda has that affect on people. She's got a good heart."

"Well, you have obviously followed in her footsteps. You have taught your daughter well, Mrs. Bergman."

My father piped in, the contempt in his voice only just under control. "What exactly do you want with our daughter?"

Marc stood in the background. His posture was straight and rigid. He was uncomfortable and he stared hard at Leonid.

"Mr. and Mrs. Bergman, I'll jump to the chase here. Giselle, whom I met a few months back, has an ability that my company is keen to explore. You could look at it as a form of medical research, for the greater good of man. She would be an invaluable asset if she were to participate in a trial we are doing back in Baltimore and, with your permission, we would love for her to consent." He was so confident.

I could not believe it. He was actually trying to sweet talk my parents. Holy shit, I could not let them get dragged into this whole mess.

"Baltimore? Oh lord, that's nearly a thousand miles away!" My mother panicked.

"Um, can we discuss this in private?" I addressed him. "Is that okay with you guys?"

My father was reluctant to leave, but my mother, who had powers of persuasion down to a fine art, finally got him to join her in the day room. "Come along, Geoff. Give her some space, just this once."

Once they had left, I flung myself at Leonid, thumping him hard in the chest. "Okay, cut the bullshit. What do you want?" I hissed.

"Giselle, is that any way to speak to someone who has your best interests at heart?"

"Oh my frigging God. Do you even have a heart? Did he put you up to this? Huh?"

"On the contrary. He has no idea where you are. Alexander is frantically searching the mountains. I think that Antoine did a very fine job of binding your charm, but of course, Antoine is no match for me."

He stood up and walked closer to me and that distinct smell hit me straight away, its odour luring me in. "It has come to my attention that things have taken a turn for the worse. I did always believe that Atarah was drawn to the darkness a little too much for my liking, but again, that was what first attracted me to her. She willingly took on the role of mother to my son, but I was blinded by her beauty and her devious plans."

I cut him off. "Right, so where do I fit in all this? I won't be a surrogate or whatever it is your friend, Vadim, foresaw. I refuse!"

"I am not asking you to be a vessel for Alexander. I am asking you to allow me to father your child. My intentions are pure. They are not perverse and dark like Atarah's. Our child would be for the greater good of man as well as the Nelapsi."

"You are so out of your mind. I couldn't do that with you. It would be like having sex with my father . . . ugh. God, no." I could not believe what I was hearing.

"I promise you, our union would be with good intention. It would not be clouded with deception. You would have full knowledge of everything that would happen."

"I can't. I'm finally having the chance to get my life back on track. Marc and I could actually make a go of things. I don't want to. I want to forget everything that has happened. You and your twisted family have screwed with me long enough. I want my life back and now that I'm home, I'm staying."

He laughed at me. His eyes glistened amber and then returned back to their previous shade. "Then tell me, wise one. How will you feed your hunger? Will your boyfriend allow you to feed from him? Is he willing to let you drink from his soul? Bear in mind that each time he would lose years from his life. You are no longer a complete human. You are one of us and that is something which can not be denied."

"What will you do if I don't agree?"

"You will agree." He was confident.

"How can you be so sure?" I tested him.

"Because if you love your family and all those you hold close to your heart, you will leave with me tonight."

Chapter 13

It was happening again. I was being forced into an impossible situation, one where I had no control over my future. I hated being so defenceless. I felt I was going insane and there was nothing I could do to prevent the inevitable happening. I wanted the ground to open up and swallow me whole. If I was going to hell, why not just take me then and there?

Leonid stood before me. He was strong and I was no match for him. Even the charm held no resistance against him. "I will give you until sunset to make your mind up. Remember, Giselle, I do not make threats lightly and as much as it pains me, I will do as I say." He left the room, passing my parents as he walked out of the house.

Inside my head, I was a mess. I wanted to protect those I loved, but how could I put a price on my own head? I did not know if I could go through with Leonid's demands. How could I do what he wanted and still remain true to myself? A child born from us would be doomed. The outcome was no longer the 'rosy' happily ever after that I was first made to believe. Either way, I was screwed.

My mother came in, her smile was weary. "Honey, is everything all right?"

"Depends on how you define all right."

My father decided it was his turn and boy, when he wanted to say something he made sure everyone listened, neighbours included. "Young lady, I do not appreciate some stranger coming into my home and telling us things about our daughter, things that even we as parents have no knowledge of. It is high time you gave us reasons for your running away and putting us through hell.

"Do you have any idea how hard this has been on us? We anticipated the phone ringing, asking us to come and identify your body. Can you even begin to imagine what that was like for us? As if we didn't have enough to deal with. Your poor mother has been back and forth from the doctors for weeks now. Test after test and her only concern has been you. Unlike you, she is not selfish. She was thinking about you, putting you before her own health."

"What?" I asked, stunned.

"Geoff, stop it, please." My mother tried not to cry.

"She needs to know. If anything, she has pushed you further over the edge. She has to take some responsibility for this whole damned mess," he pleaded with her.

"Dad! What's wrong with mom?"

"I have leukaemia," she blurted out, her face expressionless.

The room spun as I tried to comprehend what I was hearing. My mother was sick and this whole time I was busy thinking about my own selfish needs. I looked at her. She was thin and pale. The dark rings under her eyes were lightly hidden by makc-up and I could not help noticing her hands shaking. I ran into her arms and sobbed. I did not want her to die. I wanted her to have a long and healthy life. This was my fault. We had no one else to blame but me.

"I'm so sorry. Please, tell me you'll be okay."

"I . . . can't do that. I have to have more tests and treatment. We don't know if treatment will be any use. It's progressive," she cried.

I wiped my own tears from my face. "No! This cannot be happening. Daddy, please tell her that you can fix this. Please," I begged my father.

"I'm afraid this is one thing I have no control over. We have the best doctors, but we just cannot guarantee the outcome." For the first time I saw my father looking defeated, something I had never witnessed before.

"Did I do this? Did I make you ill?" I cried angrily.

"This was happening a long time before you left. It is out of our control. I'll just continue to take my meds and hope for the best, but maybe you should prepare yourself for the worst," she muttered.

"No!" I refused to accept what she was saying. "That is something I will not do."

I ran from the room, past Marc and out into the evening sun. Tears burned in my eyes as my throat ached from holding back my screams. I ran down to the shore of the lake.

Families were out together, laughing and enjoying each other. Their innocent faces mirrored memories from my past. I was once like them, completely caught up in my own world and thinking the world revolved around me. I, like many others, thought I was invincible. Bad things only happened to others, not to me or my family.

Boy, was I wrong.

It was shortly after six and I had until around nine that night to make up my mind. It felt as though I was taking part in a game of Russian roulette, and I was getting closer to pulling the trigger with the gun pointed at my own head. I did not want to leave, especially now knowing that my mother was sick. Yet if I stayed, I knew Leonid would not think twice about killing my family. I could not live with those consequences.

Marc had followed me down to the lake. He did not speak. Instead, he watched me, trying to figure out what I was going to do next.

"I suppose you heard all that. Did you know she was sick?" I asked.

"My mom told me. I think your mom confided in her a month or so ago. I'm sorry."

"What's to be sorry about? People get sick all the time."

"Yeah, but your mom is in a bad way."

"How can you be so sure, huh? She won't give up without a fight. You know her. She is Marylyn Bergman, for Christ sake. She is a force to be reckoned with," I choked.

"Giselle, there are some things even your mom can't control."

"I have to leave, you know." It came out without me realising it.

Surprised, he shoved me round to face him. "Are you crazy? You've only just got back. You can't just disappear again!"

"Who said anything about disappearing? I'll just be out of town for a while. I'm going to go with Leo, Mr. Baranski, and let them do their tests. I'm kinda obliged too."

"You have no obligation to those hounds. You didn't sign anything, so step up and do the right thing by your family." Anger filled his words.

"You have no idea what commitment I have made to these people. I wasn't thinking straight when I left and, well, I made some stupid mistakes. Now it's my duty to fulfill my obligation and don't dare lecture me on what is right or wrong. You haven't come close to earning a say in what I do."

I had hurt him. Regret drowned my heart as I watched him walk away. It was better that way. I was protecting him from the truth. If he knew what I was going to do, I think he would have taken on anything to stop me. I could not live with his death on my conscience. I loved him too much.

Behind me, a voice I knew well spoke, "I trust you have made up your mind?"

"Antoine, why didn't you stop him from coming here?" I questioned him.

"Because, sweet Princess, Leonid is not our foe. He will take on the role of Alexander. As I said before. We do not have much time and, well, you can figure out the rest yourself!"

"So you weren't really protecting me from anything. You were just safeguarding your own plans."

"No, Giselle. We were protecting you from your eventual death. This way, you get to live and see your child grow up to be a master among his followers."

"Aren't I still bound to Alex? He'll sense me with another," I asked curiously.

"Your bond cannot be broken, but the distance can weaken it. The less you consume each other, the more fragile it will become. And, of course, if Leonid successfully impregnates you, the likelihood is that your bond with Alexander will eventually die." Confidence flowed from him.

"I thought I could trust you, Antoine."

"Dear, sweet Giselle, I am the only one you can trust. Well, myself and a few others, but nonetheless, I am thinking about you and your safety. At the same time, I admit that I cannot deny my people their rightful heir."

"So I guess I am still a prisoner, right? I mean, what choice do I have?" I said through gritted teeth. "Hmm? Exactly. Just as I thought."

"Giselle, I fear that coming home has brought out the devil in you. I like this feisty side, but, alas, you do have a choice and you really ought to choose wisely. Leonid can be quite the monster when pressed hard enough."

It was all so easy for him. He had no family or sick mother to worry about. I knew I would agree and that was something that sickened me even more. I had lost my fight, but I had a request of my own.

"Okay, but I want something in return."

He shuffled uneasily, not knowing what I was going to say. "Within reason."

"I want one last night at home and I want to spend it with Marc. I want to be with him just this once. To know what genuine love feels like."

He did not answer me for several minutes. He eyed me as I anxiously waited for his approval. "Okay. You have until sunrise. And, Giselle, give me no reason to come looking for you." He left, while I stood watching the water as it trickled on the stones in front of me.

I envied those with a simple life. Without a second thought, I ran back towards the house. No one heard me as I crept in and carefully climbed the stairs to my room. I packed lightly, only taking the necessities and some pictures. I sat at my desk and brokenheartedly wrote to my mother.

Dear Mom,

I'm so sorry for all the pain I've caused you. If I had just confided in you about the whole mess with Marc maybe things would have been different. I don't know what to do. I'm bound by some crazy deal that I made when I left and there's no get-out clause. I know Daddy hates me and blames me for your illness, but please believe me when I tell you that I love you more than anything in this world. You made me a good person and I know that at times I make silly choices, but I'm still your little girl. I always will be.

Poor Ryan and Kevin are going hate me for doing this, but I've got to go. Please go easy on them. They don't make half the mistakes I do. They're great guys and you should be proud of them.

I need you to get well, because when I get back I'm going to need you more than ever. You're my backbone, Mom, and don't ever forget that.

Tell Daddy I am sorry and that I love him.

I'll be in touch as soon as I can.

I love you.

Giselle. Xxx

I left the letter sitting on my bed and walked quietly down the stairs and out of the house. Goodbyes are hard enough without the knowledge that you may never see your mother again. So I left the place I belonged and carried the burden heavy on my heart.

* * *

Walking down Elm Grove seemed to take an eternity. I passed people who were surprised to see me, but the only person on my mind who mattered was Marc. I had one chance to be with him, body and soul, and I was not willing to let anything get in my way.

I had made this same journey many times over the past four years. Not once had I ever felt this nervous. My insides twisted with the anticipation and with worrying every so often about the possibility of Marc rejecting me. I would not be able to handle that. After his being with Evie, it was now my personal mission and I had to fulfill that ambition.

When I approached the drive, I noticed that neither Richard nor Deborah's cars were home. I continued up the path, only pausing for a few minutes, composing myself before I rang the doorbell.

Breathe, just breathe!

Marc came to the door before I had the chance to press the bell. He was as surprised as I was to find I had actually gone to him.

"Err . . . hi!" I said sheepishly.

"Hi!"

"I . . . I didn't want to leave without having the chance to say goodbye properly."

"I was just heading out," he said, barely looking at me.

"Can't I come in for a minute?" I asked, trying not to sound desperate.

"Um . . . Yeah sure." He avoided making eye contact with me

I followed him inside. Our argument from before still lingered in the air and I could sense the awkwardness that was building between us. He looked gorgeous. He wore his usual distressed jeans, white t-shirt, and open shirt combo. Freshly shaven and totally irresistible.

"What do you want, Giselle?" he asked.

"I want you. No one else, just you. I can't leave with so much anger between us. I want us to clear the air, once and for all. Please." Finally, I begged.

"Okay. We're done. You forgive and well, I . . . I'm ready to call it quits. I won't be bothering you anymore."

I could not believe what he was saying. This was not going the way I had planned. I felt like a failure, but with a little more fight inside, I refused to admit defeat.

"Marc, I want to be with you tonight. I want us to be together, even if it's just this once."

I moved closer to him. My heart pounded within my chest as I touched his face. Its smooth texture felt like silk. I longed for him to touch me back. I wanted to feel the electricity flow through me and wanted to give myself to him completely.

It was not long before he looked into my eyes. My heart ached when I saw the want in his. I gently took his hand in mine and led him up the stairs to his room. We stood in silence by his bed. Nerves built up inside me as we moved closer together.

Marc drew me close to him. The aroma of his skin smelt sweet and woody and made me want him even more. I could feel his heart pick up pace as he kissed me gently. I parted my lips and the kiss intensified, becoming urgent as our tongues glided over each other. I pulled at his shirt, letting it fall into a heap on the ground. As he undone my shorts, I slipped my t-shirt over my head. His hands gently touched my back as he opened my bra, revealing my bare skin. Touching him through his jeans, I could feel how aroused he was becoming. I tugged at his belt and unfastened the fly; jeans and boxers fell to his feet.

Collapsing onto the bed, Marc was on top of me, kissing my collarbone as his sweet breath danced on the surface of my skin. His fingers explored my body as my hands ran feverishly over his back. My heart blazed like the sun as our bodies wrapped around each other, our flesh becoming one.

In time with each other, our bodies moved with eagerness. He felt so good to me. Not one moment went by when he did not look into my eyes. He watched me as he brought me close to climax, pressing his body harder and closer to me. When I reached orgasm, my body exploded like a burst of stars falling from the sky.

Marc gently moaned as his body shivered on top of me, contracting his muscles. The intensity of his climax floated into me and I tasted his energy, its fire exhilarating my very core. And then I panicked and pushed him off me. I did not want to drink from him. Confused, he lay beside me, breathless as I controlled my urge. Closing my eyes, I willed the desire for his life source to go, and slowly, I opened my eyes. Finally, I was able to rest my head on his chest, and I waited for sleep to come to me.

Listening to the sound of his heart beating in time with my own, I felt the touch of his hand against my back. His fingers gently circled around, sending a shiver down my spine.

"I love you," he whispered softly.

"I love you, too."

"Then don't go," he said with sadness in his voice.

"Oh, Marc . . . I wish I could stay, but I can't."

"Why? Surely, you can just walk away from this commitment you've made?"

I sat up, pulling the covers over my chest. "It's not that simple."

"Come on, Giselle, please. No more lies," he pleaded with me.

Grabbing a hold of his white t-shirt, I pulled it over my head and sat back down beside him, letting him wrap his arms around me.

"You wouldn't believe me."

"Try me!"

"Okay, but you won't like it," I warned him.

"I'll be the judge of that."

"Alex isn't who we think he is. Remember that guy who came round earlier? He is Leonid Baranski, Alex's dad." Confusion swept across Marc's face. "I kinda left with Alex the night of the prom. He took me in, and whilst there we kinda hooked up. Now, he wants me back and I've kinda made a promise, a favour to him and his family. They now want to call in that favour. That's all I can tell you."

I left out the bit that described them as blood-sucking monsters and incestuous and the fact that I was to have a baby who was to be a saviour to some and a dictator to others.

Marc loosened his hold on me. "You mean to tell me that you and Alex . . ."

"No. We didn't, although it was close," I lied.

"So, what is this promise you made?"

"I can't . . . I'm sorry. I know it sounds so frigging screwed up and, believe me, I don't understand it, but I'm going and there is no stopping this."

"I won't let you go," he shouted. "I'm not going to sit back on my ass when my girlfriend is being forced into something she doesn't want to do. Hell, I'll shoot the mother . . ."

"Marc, listen to me," I interrupted him. "You cannot mess with these guys. They are so deadly that you would never stand a chance. Promise me that you won't do anything stupid."

He shook his head. "Jesus, G, this is totally insane."

"Promise me, Marc. If you love me, you will do this one thing for me. Stay away."

I threw myself into his arms, crying. I felt him tremble as he shed his own tears.

"I just can't give up on you."

"Then don't . . . Just wait for me."

He did not argue with me after that. Eventually, I fell asleep in his arms.

Chapter 14

The morning light woke me. Marc was still fast asleep beside me, his breathing soft and relaxed. He looked peaceful and, intent on keeping it that way, I gently climbed out of the bed and dressed. Careful not to make a sound, I tiptoed to the side of the bed and bent down. I kissed him softly on the forehead.

"Goodbye. I will always love you," I whispered as tears filled my eyes.

Leaving the room I did not look back and silently snuck out of the house into the morning sun and the waiting car. I left what had happened behind at the door and prepared to embark on the rest of the nightmare that was to become my life.

I did not know what was becoming of my heart and mind, but one thing I was sure of was my desire to run, to run away from everything. Knowing that I was soon to climb between the sheets with my so-called 'father-in-law', I hesitantly began to pray to the Goddess. It was crazy, I know, but desperate times call for desperate measures.

Closing my mind to the present, I called Lilith forth, begging her for guidance and strength. My hand held on tight to the charm that Antoine had given me and with pure grit, I pleaded.

"Goddess Lilith, help me. Keep me patient and strong. Help me to trust your wisdom and resist the coward's way," I muttered to myself as the car moved forward.

Antoine never asked any questions and I was not about to tell him anything. He read through the morning papers, mumbling to himself and shaking his head. The Star Tribune's headlines caught my attention, *Kenwood Cyclist Dies, Children Killed Before Fire Started,* and *Youths Aged Fifteen Arrested Over Homeless Man's Murder.*

"Your humans have no regard for life. They care nothing about consequence," Antoine blurted out, laughing. "Makes one wonder why we bother killing them when they're so intent on doing it themselves. Fickle little creatures, aren't they?" He looked at me as I scoffed at his comment.

"Maybe we humans aren't perfect like you, but we have morals," I fought back.

He laughed. "Morals? Dearest Giselle, humans have long lost their moral high ground. They are answerable to no one other than the Underlord himself. After all the chaos that they cause, is it any wonder their God has turned his back on them? And remember, sweet Princess, you are no longer one of them. Must I keep reminding you of that?" He was sarcastic.

We spent the remainder of the journey in silence. I would not give him the satisfaction of getting into another debate. I had the feeling that he would always have the upper hand and, well, I hated losing, so it was better to just stay quiet.

We approached a private airstrip, east of Minneapolis-St.Paul airport. The car came to a stop outside a hangar and Antoine immediately opened the door and got out of the car. I sat back, trying to stall the next leg of the journey.

I failed.

I was practically pulled from the back of the car and forced to stand beside Antoine. We waited whilst a large man with long black hair spoke into a cell phone. He nodded and then ushered us forward.

All around me were super-sized men wearing matching black clothing. Each one had a little earpiece and talked into his wrist. It felt surreal. I could not understand all the security and curiosity always got the better of me.

"Anyone would think you were protecting the President," I sneered sarcastically.

"We may as well be. You're precious cargo."

"Me?" I asked, stunned. "Jesus Christ!"

"Who else would need the protection of The Knights of Cernunnos?" He was so pleased with himself. "Bearing in mind that you are to be our vessel, we cannot afford for any harm to come your way."

Sneering at him, I sighed, "There's that damned word again, 'vessel.' Can't you come up with something a little more original?"

"Like?" he asked, amused.

"Like . . . I don't know. The mother of the damned or something like that. Jesus, just lay off that other bullshit. It's starting to grate on me," I snapped.

Laughing loudly, he grabbed a hold of my hand. "Mother of the Damned. I like it. Now come. We have a long journey ahead and on the way, you can fill me in on your little adventure last night. I do love a good romance story."

"You're sick, you know that?" I snapped as I stepped in through the cabin door.

"I know, but you love it." He was right, though. I loved the way he teased me.

Complete luxury welcomed me as I sat down in a cream reclining chair, its soft leather fabric moulded to the shape of my body. To the left of the cabin was a mini theatre, a ceiling to floor flat screen TV playing in the background. Plush green carpet ran throughout the entire cabin. A bar stocked with all kinds of liquor took Antoine's attention.

He sat down beside me, cognac in one hand and a vial in the other. "Just a little something to kick-start the journey." He smiled and his radiant blue eyes flashed the all too familiar shade of scarlet.

Flight attendants dressed in red paced frantically up and down the aircraft, securing doors, checking drink decanters, and doing the usual security checks of their own, watching me as they passed. I felt myself flush every time I caught someone look at me.

Antoine gazed at me. He wore a smug grin on his face as he swigged from his crystal glass. "You know, you've got a particular glow about you today. Can't quite put my finger on it, but I'd say you got some last night."

"You are so crass. I swear you disgust me sometimes." I avoided making eye contact with him as I did not want him to see through me.

"Ah, crass I may be, but I, Giselle, could never disgust you."

He was so irritating. "How can you be so sure?"

"Because, unlike the others, I know things and you, my sweet Princess, will always be in my life."

"Here we go again. Riddles, bloody riddles. Why can't you just talk to me like a normal person and spare me the headache?"

He chuckled, which infuriated me further. "Where would the fun be in that? Besides, I love the fight, this battle of wills. If anything, I think you rather like it, too."

Anger flashed within me. I could feel it absorb every particle in my body. Taking him by surprise, I pounced on him. With strength I never knew I had, I grabbed him by his neck. The strong smell of his scent mixed with alcohol consumed me, its odour almost knocking me out as it filled my head.

Dizziness rapidly followed, but, fighting back, I looked deep into his eyes, keeping a tight hold of him as I hissed, "I hate you just as much as I hate Alex," I lied. "So don't flatter yourself. I would never be yours in a million lifetimes."

He laughed as I was pulled off him and led to the back of the cabin like some prisoner. "That's my girl," he chuckled to himself.

"Watch this one. She's a loose cannon," a tall, garish man bellowed as I was flung into one of the many empty seats.

Sitting there alone gave me plenty of time to think. My mother telling me she was sick kept playing over and over in my mind. How could I have been so blind? All the signs were there, I was just too caught up in my own childish problems to notice them. I regretted leaving her again without any kind of explanation. I worried that maybe I had seen my mother for the last time and my heart sank. She was not the easiest person to get along with. In fact, there were times when she was downright rude and stubborn, but she had a heart of gold and would do anything for me.

She was always there to wipe the tears away. She was always the one to give me sound advice, even when sometimes I did wonder where all her fight came from. But, most of all, she was my best friend, someone I could count on and right now, all I wanted was for her to tell me what to do in this impossible situation.

I drifted into a dreamless sleep and awoke to the thud of the plane landing. I jerked myself upright, my neck aching from the position I had been in and wearily I rubbed my eyes.

Antoine sat across from me. He looked brilliant and wore his usual grin. It annoyed the life out of me and I wanted to restart what I had begun earlier, but my plans were thwarted by one of the Knights of Cernunnos.

"Come, my lady. His Highness is waiting for you." He spoke eloquently.

I looked at Antoine, waiting for him to say something, anything that would reassure me. Instead, he said nothing, and watched me as I was led through the cabin and out the door.

The cold air hit me hard in the face. The wind blew my hair angrily over my face and I fumbled, trying to tie it back in place. Rain pelted down hard on me as I made my way to a waiting jeep. Slipping in a puddle of water, I fell to the ground, landing hard on my back. I gasped out in pain. Looking up into the overcast sky, cold rain fell into my eyes, stinging them. I lay there motionless, just willing my life away, ready to let go. Instead of succumbing to my wishes, I felt warm hands lifting me up, helping me upright onto my feet.

It was Antoine. Worried, he looked me up and down. "You know the part where I said you were 'precious cargo'? I meant that quite literally."

"Jeez, I only hurt my ass."

"Hmm, all the same, we can't take risks," he remarked sternly.

He pushed me toward the opened door of the jeep and I climbed in, wincing in pain. He followed, helping me as I secured my lap belt.

The island was vast and looked dead. Mountains and fjords passed us as we made our way uphill. The journey was uncomfortable, and I swear I thought my back was broken.

"Where are we?" I asked Antoine, who looked equally uncomfortable.

"Somewhere Alexander would never find you."

"What kind of answer is that?" I shouted over the chatter of the two men in front.

"It's the kind of answer that won't land you in trouble." He laughed. His beautiful smile and messy hair would melt any cold heart, but God, he was irritating.

"Who the hell am I going to tell? It's not as if I've been given a calling card to ring home!"

"You are persistent. We are on an island in the Southern Indian Ocean. That's all I'm giving away. The rest is up to Leonid." He folded his arms and looked out of his window.

To my astonishment, a house stood out amongst the harsh terrain that surrounded it. It was not the most beautiful thing I had ever seen, but it was certainly a welcome sight. I longed for a hot bath, dry clothes, and food. God, I needed food.

We pulled up inside a purpose built garage and like some kind of felon I was escorted from the vehicle and led inside through a large oak door. Walking in, I felt a rush of heat hit my face. Closing my eyes, I ignored my surroundings and the people in it and let the warmth of the room wrap itself around me and soothe the dampness and fatigue.

I sensed Leonid before I saw him and that same woodsy odour flowed as he got closer to me. Opening my eyes, I felt his hand upon my cheek. Gently, he rubbed the coldness and like a candle flame being relit, every nerve came alive inside me.

"I knew you would come."

He stood so close to me. I could smell the delicious scent of his blood. I craved it. Every hair on my body stood on end and I knew then that it would not take much coaxing to get me to drink from him. Many eyes were on me and my obvious desire was written on my face. Blushing, I pulled back from him and retreated to where Antoine stood.

"Mariella will show you to your room," Leonid said as he gestured for me to follow the tall, supermodel-looking woman.

Antoine gave me his trademark smile and winked at me as I followed Mariella. Walking behind her, I felt like a frump. I was wet, cold, hungry, and completely miserable. She was blonde with legs that seemed to go on forever. She wore a short, tight-fitting black dress that was cut on the bias. Her breasts were big and round, and next to me, she looked like a goddess.

She led me into an opulent room and I immediately felt out of my depth. It was delicately decorated in black and mulberry. A crystal chandelier hung low from the ceiling, its light reflected off the designs of damask flowers that spread across the walls. A black wrought iron bed was close to the window that was dressed in black voiles. Mariella walked into the bathroom, turning on the light.

"You can freshen up. You'll find clean clothes in your closet. Leonid will expect you in an hour. Don't be late," she said in a sultry French accent.

"Okay," I feebly replied.

Walking over to the side of the bed, I flung my backpack onto a nearby chair and threw myself down onto the fluffy, warm duvet. I lay there for a few minutes before I mustered up the energy to run a bath. I looked at the clock and saw that it had just gone past four in the afternoon. I had until five to get ready and, honestly, I was so wiped out from everything that had happened I was convinced I would not be able to do anything.

Still, I thought about the consequences and the deep hunger for both food and blood overwhelmed me. I ran the bath and watched the bubbles foam under the steaming hot water. Slipping the wet clothes to the floor, I stepped inside the large tub and sank down deep under the water.

The effect of the heat was amazing against my cold, damp skin and it instantly revived me. I ignored the now smouldering blemish that had been easily hidden when I drank the energy of my feeders, but it had been almost a week since my last fix so concealing the shadow was becoming more difficult. I lay there for half an hour trying to clear my mind. I had to try to forget my mother and Marc. I could not be with Leonid and have them there, ready to fill my head with more hurt and regret.

Once dried, I rummaged through the closet. I looked for something decent and not over the top to wear, but all I found were dresses and heels. I was not the kind of girl to dress up like this, and I certainly did not have the confidence to parade around here in a house full of vampires.

I decided on an emerald green chiffon dress. Its neckline was not too revealing and it came to just below my knee. I chose a pair of gold kitten heels that complemented the dress perfectly. I did not look too bad, but my hair was a mess and my complexion was not at its best. After a quick dab of mascara, blush, and gloss, I brushed my long hair and left it loose. I thought I looked presentable, maybe even pretty.

At exactly five p.m., the door was opened and Mariella walked in. She wore the same clothes and seemed surprised at my appearance. She looked me up and down and a smirk appeared. Almost casually, she handed me a box.

"Leonid would like you to have this."

I opened it and saw the most beautiful white gold and emerald green bracelet. It was the single most dazzling piece of jewellery I had ever seen. Ovals and round cut diamonds sat flawless against each other, shimmering in the light of the room. It looked incredible against my skin and set the dress off beautifully.

Mariella looked at me approvingly. "Best not to keep him waiting."

She was out of the door in a flash and I followed, trying not to break out in a sweat. Nerves were getting the best of me and my heart pounded as I walked quickly, trying my best to keep up with her. She took me to a room separate from all the others. It was situated at the back of the property and to access it, we had to walk through a long narrow hallway. Once outside the door, she knocked gently and then retreated, leaving me alone in the hall.

"Come!" I heard a voice from beyond the door.

Taking a deep breath, I turned the handle. I knew exactly what would happen between Leonid and me.

Chapter 15

Entering the room, I gasped. It was like entering a small apartment. A fire roared and the lights were dim. Leonid sat by the fire in a large ornate chair. He wore grey trousers and a black shirt open at the neck. His green eyes shimmered in the light, only a tiny hint of red flashed through them every so often. To the left of the room were two separate doors and towards the back was a large glass door that led out onto a balcony. To my immediate right, a doorway led to a small kitchenette. This was obviously his private quarters and, feeling nervous, I stood still, my feet refusing to move forward.

"Please, take a seat," he said, pointing to the empty chair in front of him.

I slowly made my way over. He got up from his seat and waited for me to sit down before returning to his previous position. "You look beautiful tonight," he said, handing me a glass of wine.

"Thank you, and thank you for the gift," I replied, gently touching the bracelet on my right wrist.

"I knew it would please you." He shuffled in his seat before moving close to the edge.

"Now that you are here, I suppose there is no point in wasting time with idle chat."

Feeling my heart race, I gulped down the liquid and to my astonishment I realised that it was not wine. I swallowed the blood and it ignited my thirst. I knew that smell, the same scent from before and looking over at Leonid, I soon realised that it was his blood. It was still warm and I knew there had to be an open wound somewhere on him.

I toyed with the idea of just going for it. Pouncing on him, searching for the line of crimson, but I knew what would follow and I was still unprepared for it. He knew what I was thinking. He saw the desire in my eyes, and without any ceremony, he stood up and removed his shirt. Just under his beautiful collarbone was a cut, only a few centimetres wide, but it was enough for me to drink from.

I cautiously stood up and did a double take of the room. The pelting rain hitting hard against the window was enough to distract me from my thirst. Looking out into the blackness, I thought about my own brooding darkness and what lay ahead of me. As I walked to the window, Leonid watched me, confused by my sudden change of heart.

"Where have you taken me?" I asked as I looked back at him.

"What does it matter? We're some place Alexander would never consider travelling to."

"It matters to me. Why can't you be honest with me for once? Please!" I asked him, my voice broken.

"We have taken you to The Kerguelen Islands."

"Oh?"

"The Southern Indian ocean. I'm sure Antoine has already given you that information."

"Well, yeah, but . . ."

"What is the problem? I promise you, there is nothing to be frightened of here. You are perfectly safe." His voice was so gentle.

I was taken aback by his honesty. I did not have to fight, scream or shout for an answer. He willingly gave me what I wanted. I could feel the glare of his eyes on the back of my head. I knew then that I was obliged to fulfill my part of the deal.

Leonid stood behind me and rested his cool hands on my shoulders. I could smell the sweetness of his breath as he whispered gently in my ear, "I promise you I will never hurt you."

Turning me around to face him, he placed his hands on either side of my face and brought his lips down to mine. They were soft and, unlike Alex, he kissed me tenderly. There was no need to rush. He had complete control of me and I let him draw me closer. Surrendering, I kissed him back, gliding my tongue over his and the taste of him rekindled the fire inside me.

As he pushed me up against the cold glass of the window, the intensity of the kiss left both of us breathless. He looked deep into my eyes, as if he were drinking from my soul and without any warning he bit into me. His fangs cut sharply into my neck and the pain left me weak. As he drank from me, I could feel my pulse race and my back arched as the familiar feelings of pleasure ran through me. I did not want him to stop. I wanted him to drink me up, devouring every last piece. I could die like this and longed for death to take me.

Pulling away from me, my blood dripped down his chin. He smiled, his thirst satisfied. Lifting me up into his arms, he carried me into one of the rooms. In the centre of the room was a four-poster bed. The windows had no drapes, allowing the stars in the sky to look in on us as though they were a million eyes.

He stood me upright next to the bed and undid the back of my dress. Soon, I fell onto the cold silk covers. Like some ancient God, he stood before me naked. His body was a marble sculpture. He was unbelievably beautiful and he wanted me. He moved on top of me as his lips caressed my naked chest. He brushed his lips over the dark shadow and refused to be startled by its presence.

My body shivered as goose pimples covered the surface of my skin. With ease, our bodies became one. Kissing me, his hands gently brushed up the side of my thigh as he pushed further into me. Gasping, I let out a gentle cry. He moved with skill and my body became his. Burning desire consumed us both. Shifting positions, I straddled him, taking him deeper into me.

My fingers traced over the line of blood under his collarbone and found it was still moist. I lowered my mouth and my tongue tasted the fresh line of crimson. Its sweet, woodsy aroma filled my head with want and lust. I slid my nail across the cut, easing the flesh open and I gently drank from him. It satisfied my thirst, only leaving my body craving more of him.

I wanted to feel more of the surge of electricity that was building up ready to explode. Slowly it kept on rising, gradually intensifying as I came closer and closer until my body could not take any more. With an explosion of ecstasy, I moaned out loud as both of us reached the peak of satisfaction.

Together our bodies trembled from the urgency of our orgasm. His hands held firmly onto my hips as his eyes remained fixed on mine. We stayed like that for a few minutes, both of us gasping for air. My heartbeat began to steady and my breathing became less rapid. Exhausted, I lay down beside him. He wrapped his arms around me and kissed me gently on my forehead.

I felt sickened by what we had just done. Guilt over my mother and Marc ran through my mind. When he touched the side of my face, a flicker of something else came to me and the thought scared the hell out of me. The last words I heard before sleep came startled and excited me.

"You're mine now."

* * *

When I awoke from my sleep, I found Leonid had gone. Beside me, a single rose lay in his place. Holding the rose between my fingertips, I sleepily got out from under the sheets and wrapping one loosely around me, I walked over to the window. The rain was still pouring, making the bleak and barren environment look even more hostile. Nothingness surrounded us and the thought of being so far away from home made me feel nauseated and completely defenceless. Yet I felt calm knowing Alex could not get to me.

From behind me a voice startled me. "I trust you have rested well?" Mariella asked.

"Yeah, I, um . . . still feel quite tired," I answered, wishing she and her Goddess body would leave me alone.

"Miss. Bergman, it is after five. Surely, you have mustered up enough energy to eat."

Her remark irritated me. "Food? Um, yeah, sure. I'll be ready in five."

"No need to rush. I have had a tray prepared for you. It is waiting for you in the lounge." She turned and left the room.

I walked over to the bed were a white silk robe had been placed. I let the sheet fall and put the robe on, tying it tightly around my waist. I walked barefoot into Leonid's lounge and saw a table had been set for me. Upon it was a choice of breads, croissants, ham, and cheese. I piled some bread and cheese on a plate and filled my cup with hot steaming coffee. Stuffing my face, I looked around the room. No pictures, no hint of his family adorned the walls. Unlike the estate in Armenia, this room felt cold and unloved. It gave me the creeps.

Finishing my coffee, I heard the door open and to my surprise Antoine walked in. He had a book in his right hand while his left held the door open.

"It is always a pleasure to see you, Giselle," he said as he bowed and a hint of devilment flashed in his eyes. "Of course, I have never seen you look as beautiful as you do now."

Swallowing the last of the coffee, I could feel my face turn a nice shade of rose.

"Oh, come on. Surely you of all people know when to take a compliment!"

"I'm not sure what you're on about, but, thanks . . . um, okay." I felt uncomfortable and wanted to pretend I had not seen him.

"Come, we have lots to do," he said.

"What? I haven't even washed yet. Can I have at least ten minutes to make myself a little more human looking?" I sarcastically blurted out.

"Mmm, for you, yes, but don't tell anyone. I don't want my staff to think I've gone soft."

He made himself comfortable in Leonid's chair and opened the book. "Well, go on then. Tick tock, tick tock..."

I gave him a scornful look and ran to the bathroom. I showered quickly, forgetting to rinse out the conditioner and tried in vain to make myself look somewhat decent. I failed, yet again. Lank, limp, lifeless hair and no make-up in sight. I felt and looked like a frump. The only thing that looked good on me was the black three-quarter-length jumper and dark blue jeans that had been left on the bed. There was no hope for my hair, so I tied it back and tried to forget that my face was a blank canvas.

Antoine was getting impatient, and his arrogance flowed when he called me. "As much as I'd like to sit here all day and wait for you, I have more pressing things to be getting on with. Bloody women!"

"Hey, I'm done! Okay, this is as good as it gets for me today." I awkwardly shuffled over to him.

Looking me up and down, he rubbed his chin. "Well, I guess you'll have to do, but that hair . . ."

"Don't. Just don't," I interrupted him, raising a finger and scowling.

Laughing, he walked up to the door and held it open for me. "Ladies first." He gestured.

"Gee, thanks," I said as I walked past him.

He was still chuckling to himself when we reached the main corridor of the house.

We passed rows of doors on our right as we moved further up the house. Stopping outside the last door, he knocked and a woman's voice answered.

"Come!"

Antoine smiled at me. "It's showtime!"

"What?" I stalled, as he opened the door.

"I'm joking. Just a little present from Leonid."

At first I did not get it, but when I walked in to the room I soon realised it was a feeding suite. A young woman sat on a leather two-seat settee. She was blonde with piercing blue eyes. She was slightly plump, but she looked healthy and her calm demeanour helped ease my own uncertainties.

"My name is Nikita. I will be your source tonight," she said in a sultry Russian voice.

"Oh! Um, are you sure?" I asked.

"But of course. Anything for his Highness," she replied.

Antoine gave another mocking bow and left the room. I stepped toward her and noticed bruising on the side of her neck. She had obviously engaged in feedings before, but I wondered how pure her essence was. She looked no more than thirty and I was pretty sure I had seen her previously, but then again it might have been just another moment of déjà vu.

"You know what will happen once I drink from you?" I asked. I was worried that she had been coerced into this, and I hated the thought of drinking from someone who did not know about the lasting effects.

"My Lady, I am well aware of what will happen to my soul, but I have much to look forward to. I will be turned if I do this for my master." She smiled at me.

"Turned? Oh . . . Oh!" I was shocked. She was willing to give up her humanity for me.

"Do not look so startled. I know what I am doing and I long for my eternal life."

"But . . ." She cut me off before I could finish.

"Please. Don't make this any harder for yourself. Drink from me and we both get what we want."

Without being pressed any further, I sat beside her and placed my hands on hers. She took a deep breath as I looked into her eyes. I could sense her innocence and it felt good. I moved my face closer and let my lips brush against hers. Instantly, I could feel her life flow into me. The essence was invigorating and it penetrated deep within me. A light was being switched on inside and I felt alive. The power left me feeling invincible and I am pretty sure I glowed. As I pulled back from her, she gasped. Her eyes seemed vacant and her breathing was rapid.

"Nikita?" I called her name. "Nikita, wake up."

She did not reply. The only sound was the rattling noise that came from the back of her throat. Her eyes slowly glazed over and rolled back and it was then that I screamed.

I ran to the other side of the room still screaming. Pulling at my hair, I started to sob. Tears flowed down my cheeks and my stomach turned. I was sick on the red rug and had no control over the retching that followed. Antoine burst into the room and realised what had happened. He called for Mariella, who came running in with a team of men. She looked at me and shook her head.

"I told you she was too inexperienced to be left alone," she hissed at Antoine.

He looked over at me, pity in his eyes. "She was not to know. It happened. Deal with it."

He came over to my side and handed me his handkerchief. I rubbed my mouth clean and got to my feet. Still sobbing, I could not find the words to speak. I could only look at the corpse of Nikita, and became aware of the fact that I was the one responsible for her death.

I ran from the room and down the long, dimly lit corridor until I came to the large oak door at the bottom of some steps. Pushing it open, I ran from the house. I kept going until I came to the edge of the makeshift road that led up to the house.

I stood shivering in the cold night air as the rain pounded down hard on me and, without a second thought, I ripped the charmed necklace that Antoine had given me from my throat and threw it into the dirt. I cried uncontrollably as my eyes burned from the harsh wind that blew in my face. I fought through my anger and despair and continued on. The further I ran, the more distant the house became. Breathless, I came to a halt at the shoreline.

The wind howled as it strengthened and squally snow hit against me, leaving me chilled to the bone. My damp clothes clung to me as I shivered. Looking around, I could hardly make out the cliffs behind me. The house was now a dot in the distance. Shock began to set in and, giving up, I fell onto the muddy ground below me. I held onto myself, shaking and crying. I had no more strength to run back to safety and now I accepted the fact that I would die out here, cold and alone.

At first, I did not hear the whispers. I only heard the wind whistling in my ears. Then the noise became more distinctive, repeating the same thing over and over. I looked around me, trying to see who was there with me. I stared into nothingness.

Darkness.

"Who's there?" I called out.

Nothing. Just the same incoherent voice calling me.

"Giselle." My name was called. Straining my eyes, I saw no one, only the small flecks of snow falling in front of me.

Panic set in as I scrambled to my feet, falling twice as I tried to balance on the increasingly slippery ground.

"Can you hear me?" The voice became louder, and clearer.

"Yes," I answered, breathless.

"Can you see me?" It spoke again.

I struggled to try to see who it was. "No! I can't." I panicked.

"You should. I'm right in front of you."

It was then that the glow of yellow eyes became clear in front of me. I could see nothing else but them. They began to multiply. All around me, shadows emerged from nowhere, their eyes glowering at me. I could feel hands pull and tug at me and looking back towards the house I saw it begin to fade. I screamed, but it was too late. The darkness had come for me and it swallowed me whole. I stood in darkness, surrounded by shadows, each one screaming for my soul.

Chapter 16

I felt as if I were floating through space. I had no control of my limbs and my voice remained soundless. I could make no sense of where I was falling, but one thing I was sure of, I was not alone.

They watched intently as I panicked. There was nothing for me to grab a hold of. Instead, I fell into what seemed like a bottomless pit.

I found it hard to breath. The air was stale and the stench of death burned at the back of my throat. With a jolt, I found myself standing in the centre of a small room. A wooden bed pressed up against a wall, bars formed the shape of a door in front of me and the echo of screams tormented me.

I thought I was in hell.

I felt totally dejected.

Would I be trapped here forever in this demonic existence?

Sitting down on the bed, I waited for someone or something, but no one came. I have no idea how long I sat there, whether it was minutes or hours or even days. I lost all sense of time and felt like I would finally lose my mind.

Out of nowhere, it appeared in front of me like a cloud of darkness, only this was in the shape of a man. His eyes glowed a frightening shade of yellow and immediately, I closed my eyes, trying to avert my gaze. I did not want to stare into the abyss any longer.

"We have been patient," it slurred. "Now the time has come for you to complete your phase."

Confused, my eyes burst open. More eyes stared at me, their features non-existent. "What do you want from me?" I asked, trying not to let fear fill my words.

"You and the child," it hissed.

"Me? My . . . child? I don't have a child."

Laughing, the glow from the eyes came close to my face and I could feel its hand rest on my abdomen. "Mmm, only time will tell." He looked down from my face and rested his eyes on my chest. Looking back up at me, he sneered, "But of course, we have ways of finding out and, believe me, chosen one or not, you will wish death rather than have one of my minions have his way with you."

Their laughter bellowed through my ears. I screamed and continued doing so until my voice was raw. I was left alone in their world with no one else to turn to. I begged Lilith to bring me some kind of peace. She owed me that much and if I was to die here, then I wanted it to be at her hands and not at the hands of the creatures of the damned.

"Goddess Lilith, I beg of you, please, open the channels and set my soul free. If I am to die, be it your will. Open the gates and carry me home," I chanted over and over.

"Your words will do you no good, you know!" A voice came from beyond the barred door.

Walking up to the doorway, I peered out into the darkness. There was nothing. I stood there for a few moments, holding my breath, trying to make out noises or anything that gave me a clue to where it was.

"It's scary, isn't it? The darkness?" The voice spoke again.

"Who are you?" I whispered.

"I am nothing. I am just an echo from the past and a dot in the future."

The words scared me. "Don't say that. I think I'm depressed enough."

"The darkness will drink you up. Every last bit of you will succumb to it. Of course, that will only happen once you have given birth."

Shaking my head in protest, I shouted, "I won't be having a kid, okay! Not here, not ever!"

"I beg to differ. I believe the hands of fate have already begun to work." He slowly appeared before me, Afanas.

"What the . . . ? Oh my God . . . How?" I yelled at him, astonished by his presence.

"Questions, questions, questions. My dearest Giselle, must you always be so impertinent?" he asked through gritted teeth. "You should be thanking me."

"What? Are you serious?" I bellowed at him.

"They wanted to kill you straight away, but as always I used my powers to great effect. I managed to put your

execution on hold, for the time being anyway." He raised his
eyebrow, clearly delighted with himself.

"But why, Afanas? I thought you were my friend,
someone I could count on," I cried.

"Who is to say that I am not?" he questioned me.

"But this place . . ."

"Ah, yes. This isn't the standard you are accustomed to,
but, rest assured, things will change."

My legs finally gave in and I fell onto the cold, damp
floor. "I just don't get it. Why are you even here?"

"Because it was I who summoned the shadows to take
you, to infect you with their darkness. Hence the increasing
mark on your breast. Unfortunately, I misunderstood the
importance of you and your newly found powers. I cannot
say for sure that my plan to save you will work, but I can
promise you this, you will not bring your child into this
world."

"But I'm not pregnant . . ." I began.

"Dear sweet Princess, the seed has been planted. I can
smell the scent of new life growing within you." He paused
and looked at me, his eyes a deep crimson. "Of course, we
don't want 'them' to discover this just yet. However, you
will not be able to disguise your growing body for much
longer."

"No, this cannot be happening. I had my period and,
well, me and Leonid, you know, only did it the once." I was

embarrassed by my revelation and I could see the surprise on Afanas' face.

"Ah, so it is true. Your union was consummated. Nevertheless, you are with child. That is something you cannot deny and, given time, your body will allow you the luxury of feeling that life grow within you." He was serious.

"What about Alex? He's going to be pretty pissed with us both," I said as I held onto the bars of my cell.

"Indeed, his Lordship will be most angry. And I dare say he will figure it out. He will find you, Giselle, but until then, I shall try to keep you safe." He turned to leave.

"Afanas, one last thing," I called after him.

"Yes?"

"Why did the shadows want to kill me?" I asked him yet again.

"For you to be reborn. You are to be their queen, Giselle." He disappeared and left me pondering on what he had just revealed.

I was not ready for any of it. I paced in my cell, thinking, making plans of escape, anything to occupy my mind and forget about what Afanas had told me. I could not be pregnant. I felt no different and if I was, who was the father?

Holy crap! I suddenly remembered my one and only time with the love of my life, Marc. We had not used any protection at all and I know it sounds stupid, but I did not think I could fall pregnant after my failed attempt with Alex.

A warm feeling travelled through me as I thought of the prospect of having Marc's baby. I know that it was probably a naive thing to do, but it filled me with hope, hope that I had not felt in a while. Just thinking that my baby would have a chance at a normal life gave me a sense of relief and with that thought, I lay down on the bed and fell asleep.

* * *

My dreams were filled with so much craziness. One minute, I was back in my childhood, playing on the swings with my brothers. The next, I was in a fever, screaming and pushing at people that surrounded my bed. My voice echoed as I struggled to make sense of what I was saying.

Spooked, I woke up and felt disgusting. Sweat had saturated me so much so that my clothes stuck to my skin. I craved the warmth of a hot bath. My stomach ached from hunger and, most of all, the sorrow I felt over the death of Nikita haunted me.

The touch of a hand startled me from my contemplation. It rested on my back as I lay still, frozen in my sleeping position, too afraid to turn around. I pretended to sleep as the hand rubbed along the base of my spine. Goosebumps spread across my flesh as I fought hard to remain still and lifeless.

I shuddered at the touch and then a voice spoke to me. "We have waited so long for you. The excitement is almost too much to bear," the voice slurred.

Turning round, its eyes were fixed on me, wide and golden. "I want to go home," I whispered. "Please."

"But you are home, Giselle."

"No! I don't belong here . . . in this . . . this other world. I belong with my family," I pleaded.

"You belong with us. We are your family now." His face began to emerge before me.

A middle-aged man resembling Afanas sat by my side. His back was hunched over, his expression was serious and his face was long. His eyes glowed like the sun setting, a burnt orange shade. He looked human, but I knew he was anything but. I could sense something menacing about him and I did not trust a word he said.

"Of course, you already know that, don't you? You knew you would come home one day. You wear the mark firmly on your soul." He placed his hand between my breasts. "You have always walked with darkness and now it is time to embrace it. Let it fill your heart and you will be at one with us, your most reverent servants."

"I . . . refuse. Okay? I don't want to be a part of this nonsense," I shouted as I tried to push him away from me.

"It has already begun. You will be our Queen." He held me by my throat up against the bars of my cell.

Gasping, I fought back. "I . . . will . . . not!"

I drew in my breath sharply, choking as I fell to the floor. Dizziness came first and then the unconscious world claimed me as I lay in a heap on the cold, wet ground of my cell.

Incoherent noises pulsated through my head as I struggled to regain consciousness. Screams and sounds of torture resounded as I wandered the corridors. It was like entering a labyrinth, an endless maze of tunnels that left me confused. I never seemed to get far from where I started and then suddenly I was back at the start, only each time my outward direction had changed.

From behind the walls, I could hear the desperate cries of women as they pleaded for their lives. Other staccato sounds pierced my head, making me scream as the deafening pitch seemed to burst my eardrums. I stood in silence, unable to hear my own voice. Everything had become muffled, but one voice I could hear and recognized.

Nikita.

She pleaded, as their laughter drowned out her cries. "I shouldn't be here. Please, please... No..." Her bloodcurdling scream echoed from the walls.

Her voice was all around me and its anguish buried itself inside me. I was unsure from which direction it had come, but I followed my gut instinct and headed towards a secluded tunnel. Dimly lit torches flickered as I walked in the direction of Nikita's increasing screams. Beneath my bare feet, rats rushed past. My feet sank down into the mucky ground and its putrid smell repulsed me. The closer I came to the source of the screams, the harder it was to walk through the increasingly thick muck. I could feel warm liquid ooze over my toes as I neared the end of the tunnel.

Feeling confident, I lifted up my foot and tried to climb over some barbed wire that had come loose from the wall, but I fell and cut my heel. I struggled over the rest of the wire and sat on the dusty soil inspecting my foot. Maggots and worms wriggled and fell to the ground from my legs and ankles. Screaming, I frantically tried to brush them off, squashing some into the dirt with my hands.

I was back on my feet, and I continued to follow Nikita's now deafening cries. Her wailing sent a shiver through me. It was harrowing. There was a hollow wall to the left of me, and I walked into a room that looked like a medieval torture chamber with hooks, chains, and a chair with spikes covering the seat, back and arm, leg and footrests. A triangular shaped seat was in the corner of the room, its tip covered in bloodstains.

My eyes felt as though they were bursting out of my head when I saw Nikita. Her arms were bound behind her back. A rope had been tied around her wrists and was attached to some kind of winch. She was hanging by her arms and weights had been tied to her feet. Her flesh had been ripped open. It was a horrific sight. It made me sick. I lost all sense of reality as I tried to get to her to free her, but some kind of force field held me back. I could not go any closer. I was a mere spectator.

Lifting her head, she looked around the room. When she saw me, her eyes fixed on me and she screamed, "You did this. You condemned me! You are darkness." Her voice broke, slowly her breathing became laboured and, just as I had witnessed before, she died.

In front of me, four sets of glowing eyes appeared, each one making incomprehensible noises. They moved closer to me, breaking through the force field. I screamed as I was pulled further into the room.

A hand held my head back as it spoke into ear. "Do you see why you belong here? You bring death. You are death."

* * *

Screaming, I awoke on the ground within my cell. I was cold and wet and trembled from the shock of what I had dreamt. It felt so real and for a moment, I was convinced that it was. The guilt I felt after seeing Nikita again took me further into depression. It had been bad enough the first time, but seeing her die a second time made me condemn myself even more. She was right. I was to blame and the darkness that had possessed me was the reason. I was tainted and no amount of goodness was going to erase the shadow from my soul.

Time passed before I saw anyone again. I was left cold, dirty, hungry, and alone. The sickness was the worst. It came in waves of dizziness and with it came bouts of vomiting. I honestly thought I was going to die.

I had just about given up when the door of my cell was unlocked. It swung open and in walked an old man carrying a tray. Avoiding eye contact, he set the tray beside me, stepped backwards, and left. The door remained open and I thought for a split second about making a run for it. I stayed. I had no energy for battle and I sure was not ready to meet what lay beyond my cell.

I inspected the tray. Some toast and fresh fruit had been prepared for me. There was also a goblet, full and warm, and instantly, I knew what was in it. Without giving it a second thought, I grabbed the goblet and drank the warm, thick liquid, feeling it slip down the back of my throat until the goblet was empty. I savoured the taste. It was not like Alex or Leonid, but it sure was good. It satisfied the increasing thirst that I had tried hard to ignore. Tucking into the fruit and toast, I did not pay much attention to the spectator that had taken up permanent residence at the end of my bed.

"Are you hungry too?" I asked, throwing a piece of toast in the direction of the dark brown mouse.

It did not hesitate. It picked up the piece of food and started to nibble on it. It made me smile. I was not alone, after all. A short time later, Afanas returned and brought with him some clothes and basic essentials. He paused, looking at me.

"I do believe you look rather peaky today. Are you feeling okay? Were the refreshments to your liking?" he asked as pleasantly as he could.

"Yeah. The food was great, the blood even better. I'm just not feeling one hundred percent. I think it's the lack of daylight and the need to be a bit more sanitary, but otherwise, I'm just great." Sarcasm flew with the last few words.

"Mmm, not much I can do about the sunlight. However, I believe these may be of some use to you," he said.

He handed me jeans, a sweatshirt, socks, and underwear. The toiletries were fabulous. My favourite coconut shampoo and conditioner combo were accompanied by my toothbrush, toothpaste, some hair serum, gloss, body moisturizer, and my favourite Lancôme perfume.

I smiled.

"Ah, you are so much more beautiful when you smile," he commented.

"Thank you. I didn't expect any of this." I was so overcome with emotion that I cried.

"Shush, come now, dearest Giselle." He put his arms around me. "As I've said before, do not burden yourself with tears. They do not help. You must stay strong. I will do all I can, but you must help me."

"How, Afanas? How can I do anything when all I do is sit here alone hour after hour? I don't have the strength any more. Besides, I stink like a vagrant and have the worst case of dog breath ever." I tried to laugh.

Afanas tried his best to console me. It was pointless. I was so consumed by my own miserable existence that I did not realise how sincere he was being. He got up from beside me and made his way to the door.

Turning back to me, he said, "Remember, Giselle, you are bigger than this. I know that none of this was of your choosing, but you must find the strength and courage to see this through. I believe that you are a lot stronger than you give yourself credit for and in time, you will overcome your weaknesses and you will find great power."

I sat there, dumbfounded by his confidence in me. I was not sure if I wanted to laugh or cry, but one thing I was sure of, and that was my friendship with Afanas.

Chapter 17

I had once read in one of my father's many books that, 'In the darkest hour the soul is replenished and given strength to continue and endure.' I used to think it made no sense whatsoever, but now after hearing what Afanas had said, I believed that I was in my darkest hour and needed my soul to restore itself. Somehow, I was going to achieve that. Of course, I had no clue as to how I was going to do it, but I had to trust my instincts. Not forgetting Afanas' promise to assist me, I felt a jolt of courage surge within me.

A few hours later, the door to my cell opened and in came the shadow, his eyes glaring at me. He stood at the foot of my bed, watching me as I scuffled further back. Another set of eyes came in behind him, his silhouette less visible but his eyes more menacing. They both remained silent, peering at me. They made me feel uncomfortable and almost forgetting my earlier promise to myself, I scrambled off the bed and stood just inches away from the first shadow.

"What do you want?" I asked him.

He chortled to himself and then speaking to the other, he mocked me. "And this is supposed to be our Queen."

"If I am to be your Queen, then maybe you ought to show me some respect," I angrily retaliated.

"How can we? You are a joke. Look at you. When was the last time you saw your own reflection?"

"Well, let's see . . . I have been kept here, in this damp shit hole for a while now, so I guess you know the 'facilities' aren't exactly crying out for an award anytime soon. Maybe if I was treated to the simple luxury of a toilet and shower then perhaps I would be more presentable. Or don't you want your Queen to have access to the world that lies beyond that door?" I hissed as I made my way to the door.

"That lot there." I pointed to my clothes and toiletries lying on the bed. "Bring it with you. Now, are you going to show me where I can wash or do I have to figure it out myself?" I asked the second shadow. His eyes glowed as though they were on fire.

He looked at the one behind me and without pausing for more than a moment, he walked out into the dimly lit tunnel. I followed him with a feeling of déjà vu. Eerily, the tunnel reminded me so much of the dream I had had where I found Nikita, but I put her and all my problems to the back of my mind and concentrated on the present. I had to figure out the layout of the tunnels.

I was escorted through a stone built corridor that eventually brought us to what seemed to be a building of some sort. Once we were through the door, it was closed with a bang. I was led further up some stairs that spiralled round and round. Looking down over the handrail, I felt dizzy. We were so high up.

"Where is this place?" I whispered as I looked up. The stairs seemed to go on forever.

There were no windows and the air was hot and sticky. I did not like it one bit. Finally, we came to a stop. The shadow in front of me turned around. His gaze met mine and the menacing look that he first had, had mellowed to a mere amber glow.

"You will find everything you need through those doors," he said.

The other one handed me my clothes and wash bag. I did not hesitate and as soon as I was through the door, I collapsed in a heap on the wooden floor. The dizziness was the worst than it had ever been. I felt as though I was on a boat in the open sea, waves tilting it back and forth, but the sickness that followed was uncontrollable. Each time I thought I had finished, more would come.

I can honestly say that I had never felt so sick, ever. I lay on the floor for a while, waiting for it to pass, and eventually it did. I looked around me, trying to gather the strength to get onto my feet. I was in a big bathroom. It was pretty basic, but to me it was luxury. I picked up my clothes and set them on a mahogany bench beside the bathtub. I unpacked my shampoo and conditioner and set them on the bath.

Turning on the taps, I heard a noise coming from the pipes and they creaked as the water came spitting out. Lovely hot, steamy water began to fill the bath. The mirror above the vanity unit began to steam up, but I was still able to make out my reflection. I looked a mess. My hair was dirty and tatty. My face was pale and I was pretty sure I could see the beginnings of a pimple. I looked gaunt and the shadows under my eyes made me look decidedly unhealthy.

Shrugging my shoulders, I began to peel off the filthy clothes I had worn ever since I had arrived here. They smelt bad and my underwear was useless. I threw them towards the corner of the room, adamant that I would never wear them again.

I turned around and picked up a soft blue towel from the sink. As I looked down at my naked body, I was startled by the growing dark stain that had now spread from my breast down to my navel.

Trying to reason with myself, I put the ever-growing darkness down to me being held against my will, but I was denying the truth. I knew what it meant and I was only too willing to forget that I was destined to be some kind of Queen for these shadow creatures.

Sinking into the hot water eased the ensuing nausea. My head felt light and I could hear my heart pounding, its pace increasing as I fought to stabilize my breathing with long, deep breaths. Finally, it passed and I could relax again. Letting the water spill over my head, I sank down under the water. It cleared my mind of all its woes and momentarily, I felt normal, or at least as normal as I could be, given my situation.

A knock at the door brought me to my senses. I swallowed a mouthful of the water as I bolted to the surface, drenching the wall and floor.

Coughing, I shouted towards the door, "Yeah?"

There was no response, only another knock. "Jesus Christ," I muttered to myself as I hesitantly stepped out of the tub and wrapped the towel around me.

On opening the door I saw that an envelope had been slipped underneath it. I picked it up and held it in my right hand as I peered out into the poorly lit hall. There was no one. The only sound I could hear was me, my breathing and my pounding heartbeat. I closed the door behind me and sat down on the bench. When I tore the envelope open, out fell a key and a small piece of paper.

I read the letter.

Dear Sweet Giselle,

Here is a key, a tiny piece of a puzzle that is much bigger than both of us. I know you did not ask to be involved in any of this and I reverently regret what I have done to you.

Now you must find the courage to seek the door that bares the mark of Eve. There you will find the doorway that will lead you back home, but beware of the dark ones. They mean you harm and do not believe you are the daughter of Samael.

Please, be vigilant on your journey. I will try to keep a watchful eye over you. However, I must remain here, opposed to your freedom. I must fulfill my side of the deal.

Be safe, child, and may the Goddess be with you.

Your friend,
Afanas

Sitting in silence, I held the key and stared at it. Its oval-shaped head had pretty red flecks sparkling through it. Pondering on what Afanas had instructed, I dressed quickly and, storing the key in my pocket, I left the room and proceeded to find the door that would take me home.

It was all like some bizarre illusion. Never in my wildest dreams would I have ever imagined anything like this happening to me, your average girl next door. I was never one for vivid dreaming and, to be honest, I thought for a moment that maybe my mind had been playing tricks on me and none of this was real.

Maybe it was post-traumatic stress over the Marc and Evie 'thing,' but then again, the way my stomach turned was all too real for me. The dizziness and nausea just kept on coming. One moment, I was fine and the next, I was heaving my guts up against some wall. All I wanted to do was crawl into my bed and have my mother bring me some of her homemade chicken soup. To have those special moments back would be worth every bit of pain and torment I had gone through.

My eyes filled up when I thought of my mother. She was going through her own hell and I was not there to help her, to look after her. I had been denied that the instant Leonid had stepped inside our home. Nothing would ever be 'normal' again and that was something I was going to have to learn to accept.

I soon found the stairwell that I had been escorted up from my cell. I looked down and was instantly shocked by the height. I was at least a hundred feet high and the thought of falling down into what seemed like an endless stairwell scared the hell out of me. It wound down like a vortex and as I looked upwards, it was exactly the same way, an endless spiral that continued upwards further into the darkness.

Ignoring the urge to give in and wait for whoever would come for me, I thought about my mother and Marc and, of course, Leonid and Alex. I could not help but wonder whether this had all been my destiny. If it was, why had it taken so long to materialize?

I kept this line of thinking as I wandered further up searching for doors, until I came to a stop four flights up. I could hear the murmurs of voices coming from further down a corridor. And, as always, curiosity got the better of me. I tiptoed towards the door and, holding my breath, I listened in on the conversation.

"You've felt the mark for yourself. You know she is the chosen one," Afanas said.

"I still am not confident that she is strong enough. She is too emotional. I don't think she will be able to let go of her human form very easily."

A voice I didn't recognize answered. "Ah, but you forget, old friend, she has the capabilities of my people. She is unique. Do not underestimate her power."

"Yes, Afanas, we are very well aware of her newfound power. After all, she did send us the corrupt soul of that poor girl. What was her name?"

"Nikita," Afanas said.

"Oh, yes, Nikita. The vampire whore who thought she would be turned in favour of her essence. What a silly little girl she was," he sneered.

"Then what is the problem, Xavier?" Afanas asked.

"Old friend, I believe you know the answer to that one yourself."

"Given time, we will know if the seed was planted."

"Time may be one thing we have, but in order for us to bring her to her rightful place she must fulfill the final phase. She must bear the child."

"Then we must proceed with methods that are unknown to man," Afanas said glumly.

"Indeed, Afanas. It is time for methods of the old. I shall send Rimane to bring the girl to me," Xavier said as he made his way to the door.

I scurried back down the corridor and fled up the next flight of stairs. Breathless, I stopped and tried to gather my thoughts. Afanas told me to look for 'the mark of Eve.' This was something that completely stumped me.

What was the mark of Eve? Did Afanas mean Eve as in the biblical Eve? I guess that was something I was going to have to find out.

I hid in the darkness as the shadow creatures rushed past. They were too busy to notice me lurking in the corner. I held my breath, trying not to exhale. Once the commotion had finished, I ran toward the next flight of stairs. This time, I concentrated on each floor, searching for some kind of symbol that reminded me of Eve. I had decided that it was most likely to be the biblical form of her, although that really left me no wiser, but I thought that maybe it would be something like the image of a woman upon the door. It was as good a guess as any.

Climbing further up the stairwell, I came to a large circular-shaped hall. I noticed four white doors positioned like the four points of a compass. They were very different from the dark doors I had seen below. The hall was completely empty and, being cautious, I crouched down behind a wide iron mirror that was oddly placed just to the left of the first door. I waited for a few minutes, eager to see if anyone would pass by, but nothing happened. Not one person or shadow passed through any of the doors.

Finally, I decided that I had waited long enough and walked out from behind the mirror. It was a bright hall, beautiful and angelic looking, which was bizarre considering I was in some kind of hell. Light glistened around the room as I strolled towards the first door.

Looking at the faces of the doors, I noticed that they were all identical, the only difference being their handles. Although all were round and brass, a different letter was engraved on each. Closer inspection revealed that the first door directly behind me had the letter 'S'. To the left of me was the letter 'E'. Directly opposite that one was 'W', and the door to the top of the hall had the letter 'N'. Perhaps my idle comparison of the doors being points of the compass had not been so idle after all, but none of them had anything else that I could see on them and certainly no symbols that matched the description Afanas had given me. I felt jaded.

Sitting in the centre of the hall, I slumped my head into my hands and sighed. I had been defeated. There truly was no way of escaping this place. With the key in my hand, I was ready to give up and take the long journey back down and face whatever was coming to me. Giving in was now something I was getting used to and it definitely sucked to be me.

Chapter 18

From the corner of my eye, I could see something in the reflection of the mirror. It sparkled and danced across the glass. Turning my head round, I was both shocked and excited by what I could see.

It was the reflection of a woman, her modesty protected by leaves. Her hair was long and golden, and she was unlike any woman I had seen before. She stood in front of the door that had the letter 'N' carved into it. Looking back at the door, I could see nothing was there, but through the mirror I could see Eve.

I used the mirror on the three remaining doors. The door that had 'W', carved, had the image of fire, shadows and screaming faces. Opposite it, the door with the letter 'E' had images of spirits, their faces were white and godlike, but the door that bore the letter 'N', remained blank. Nothing showed up.

I fiddled with the key between my fingers and toyed with the idea of looking behind each door even though I knew it was a risk I could not afford to take, especially now that I might be so close to breaking free. I remembered Afanas's warning not to trust the dark ones and I did not want to take the chance in running into any of them any time soon.

Calmly, I walked up to the door with 'N' engraved on it and put the key into the lock. As I turned it, I heard a commotion from the stairs. I spun round and saw a small army of shadows making their way up towards me.

"She's here," roared the shadow closest to me.

"Sound the alarm," another beckoned.

Before they came any closer, I had turned the handle and stepped through the door with no clue of where I was going or how I would get home. I closed the door with a bang and frantically turned the key, locking it from inside.

Inside? I was outside. I had left behind the hall and, in fact, the whole gloomy building. Frantically, I ran through the trees and overgrown hedges that surrounded me. I had no idea where I was, but something told me I was going to find out soon enough. The further I ran, the more familiar the area became. I recognized the willows and the scents of the wild flowers. Water rushed down the stream and the bridge was soon in my sight. It was my worst nightmare. The door had sent me back to the mountains of the Utmish Ato-tem. I was back in Armenia.

"Shit!" I whispered as I approached the bridge that lay at the foothills of the coven.

"This could only happen to me," I said as I kicked a pile of leaves that lay beside some rocks.

Sitting in the late evening sun, I looked up the hill and saw the outer boundaries of the estate. I knew that nightfall would soon descend upon me and I did not want to be left outside and unprotected. There was only one thing I could do and even though it killed me inside, I knew I had to take refuge within the coven and face Alex and Atarah. My life sucked big time and I was not expecting it to get better any time soon.

The climb up hill was a struggle in itself. I did not remember it being this bad the last time, but then again, the last time was a weird experience by all standards. I had had my first glimpse of the shadow creatures and was then rescued by Leonid. As a result of the whole damned situation, the damned mark on my chest grew darker each day.

My stomach churned as I stepped closer the outer wall. I knew now that there would be no turning back. Alex would have sensed me by now and something inside told me that he was already waiting for me. Without further delay, I stepped through the thick wooden gate and walked past the orange trees into the courtyard where my welcoming committee was ready to meet me.

Atarah and her mother, Angelika, stood beside the group of elders who had performed the blessing at my consecration. Alex stood at the front, his eyes blazing amber. I could instantly sense his rage and I knew he wanted to kill me.

Without a second thought, I did the only thing I could think of. I ran into his arms and held on tight to him. Not needing much effort, tears left my eyes and fell down my cheeks.

"Alex, you wouldn't believe what they were going to do to me," I sobbed, putting on my best performance.

He was rigid and I knew he had his doubts. His anger flowed into me as I held on tight. I was too afraid to look into his eyes and kept my eyes closed.

"Where have you been?" he asked bitterly, pushing me away from him. He placed his hands on either side of me and squeezed hard. "Don't lie to me. Where. Have. You. Been?" he roared into my face.

This time my tears were real. I was frightened and I could barely speak. Shaking me, his face became twisted. His rage was about to erupt and screaming from both pain and fright, I cried out, "Hell . . . They took me to hell!"

Confusion spread across his face. He looked back towards Atarah who calmly stood with one finger pressed against her chin. She nodded and turning back to me, he asked, "Who took you?"

"The shadows. They came and took me and I was so scared." I fell back into his arms.

This time he embraced me and tried to calm me down. "No need to worry now. You're safe. You're home!"

The words sent a wave of fear through me. Coming to my senses, I broke free from his arms. I wanted to hit him, to spit in his face. Hell, I wanted to rip his throat out.

"Where were you? Did you even try to find me?" I shouted.

I clenched my fist and hit him as hard as I could across his face. My wrist hurt from the impact, but the adrenalin was now flowing and I did not want to stop. I had to release all of my pent-up anger and this was the best and only way. It was my turn to toy with him.

"Do you even love me, huh?" I asked through gritted teeth. "Most 'husbands' would travel to the ends of the Earth and back to find the love of their life, but no, not Alexander Baranski. No, he'd rather sit back on his friggin' ass, waiting for her to come to him! Have you any idea what I've been through?"

"Enough!" he shouted. "We'll discuss this in private."

I chortled. "Private? Don't make me laugh. If I remember correctly, nothing we do stays between us."

"Don't be so childish."

"Excuse me? Are you serious? Look at me, I am a child!" I pushed past him and walked through the crowd that had gathered.

"Where are you going?" he roared.

"To bed!" I shouted back at him and continued walking until I was away from their gaze.

I closed the front door behind me and ran up the stairs to the room I had shared with Alex. Everything remained the same. My room was exactly the way I had left it, messy, but the bed looked inviting and all I wanted to do was sleep.

I stripped off my clothes as I made my way to the bed, but nausea overcame me. I ran to the bathroom and heaved until there was nothing more I could bring up. Defeated by my own body, I lay on the cold bathroom floor and waited for the spinning to stop. I did not know what was happening to me. I felt weak and I believed I could not possibly feel any worse than I did at that moment. I have no idea how long I lay there, but finally the spinning faded and I was able to lift my head from the ground.

Alex stood by the doorway, watching me as I struggled to get to my feet. His face was stiff and his expression was severe. I stumbled as I clung onto the basin. The dizziness continued and with it came a heat as though I was burning up from the inside. I was really struggling to cope with the illness, when he came from behind me and lifted me up into his strong arms. I gave in quite easily as I had no strength left in me. I was simply exhausted.

Alex smelt wonderful. The same delicious odour I had become accustomed to oozed from him. I easily lost my senses around him and even though I knew I did not love him, I could not help but crave him.

He set me down gently onto the bed and drew the covers up over me. He sat beside me and took my hand in his. His skin felt amazing against mine, almost as though it was healing me.

"Sleep, Giselle. You need your rest." His voice was smooth and silky.

And finally, I fell into a dreamless sleep.

* * *

The wind and rain stirred me from my sleep and as I sat up, I could see Alex sitting in a chair by the window. He watched me as I fidgeted with the covers. I felt uncomfortable and his continuous gaze made me feel like diving back under the blankets just to escape his eyes.

I reached over for the glass of water that had been set beside me on the bedside locker. The covers fell, revealing my underwear. Flustered, I pulled them around me and took the glass, taking a long drink.

"I can smell him on you," Alex said, breaking the long silence between us.

I froze.

"Who?" I asked him, trying my best to remain clueless.

"Oh, Giselle, must we always play these games? You allowed my father to take control of you. He and you . . . Do I really have to spell it out?" he said, shaking his head.

"Alex, I . . ."

"Don't do it. Do not lie to me." He got up from the chair and walked up to the side of the bed. He looked so angry, and I did not know how long I would be able to keep the pretence up.

"Did you let him drink from you?"

"Yes," I said, giving in. Because of our bond, he knew I was lying. He could feel my heart racing and knew from my scent that something had been altered.

"I didn't want to. It was all crazy and Antoine . . ." I held back my tears.

"Antoine? What has he got to do with all this?"

"I don't know, Alex. All I know is that I can't take any more of it. It's killing me. It's making me ill. You, your family, this whole life . . . it's not for me. Can't you just let me go, please?" I begged him.

Laughing, he ran his hand through his hair. "You are my wife and your place is here with me. There is no other life for you now. Besides, you are sick because you haven't fed properly. You look a mess and, to be honest, the smell has got to go."

I sniffed at my arm and did not notice anything unusual, but then again, Alex had heightened senses compared to mine. He would notice any difference in me.

"Aren't you angry with me?" I asked as I got out of the bed.

"What do you suggest I do? Kill you? Kill my father? Or maybe, I should kill your dying mother. Would that punish you enough?"

I was sickened by him bringing my mother into our fight. He had no right. "How could you say that about my mother? She isn't dying. She's just unwell."

Pushing past him, I went into the bathroom and began to run a bath. He followed me in and stood in the doorway, ready for round two.

"From what I hear, dear old Marilyn hasn't got long left." He was taunting me.

"Screw you," I shouted, getting ready to hit him.

He chortled as he approached me. "I remember a time when women obeyed their husbands. Back then, women knew their place, but evolution and all its graces have allowed you to become disobedient little whores. I promise you now, Giselle, with every breath in my body, I will destroy you if you ever speak to me like that again. I am your master, your commander, and I will be obeyed. Do you understand me?"

Of course, me being me, I had to retaliate. "Go. To. Hell," I spat in his face.

I did not see what was coming next. With a crash, I was thrown into the glass of the shower door. The full impact had me on my back, lying on shards of broken glass. I could feel warm liquid escape from me, but before I could inspect my wounds Alex had me pinned up against the long mirror that hung on the wall and began to tighten his grip around my neck. He was choking me.

I could feel the pulsating throb of my heart as oxygen fought to circulate around my body. It was getting harder to breath and I could feel myself losing the battle. He was winning, as my life began to drain from my body. Before I finally lost consciousness, he loosened his grip on me and I fell to the floor. I lay there bleeding. My wounds stung and I gasped for air.

He crouched down beside me and pulled my head back. "Death would be an easy option, but for now I think I'll hang on to you."

He let go of me and then unconsciousness came and claimed me.

Chapter 19

I could hear the faint sound of voices as I fought the pain that had consumed me. I knew that I was not dead, yet the burning pain made me wish for death. The voices kept repeating themselves, over and over again.

"She has lost too much blood," one said.

"She may not survive," another spoke.

"You better make sure she does survive or it's your life on the line," Alex said with contempt in his voice.

I lay motionless, unable to move or speak. The only connection with the world was through my faint heartbeat that skipped every couple of minutes. I knew I had lost a lot of blood, but I did not realise I would feel like this. It was surreal, as though I was living outside my body. I could see everything going on around me.

Three medics worked on me desperately. One stitched my back as one tended to the tears in my scalp and another pumped blood into me via a drip. By looking at all the bloody swabs that lay on the ground, I could see that I had lost more blood than I first anticipated. I was in a bad way.

My poor body no longer looked like mine and for the first time, I was afraid of how I would eventually look. I did not want to look like some freak. Things were bad enough that I drank blood and people's souls, but to look like one, well, that was another story.

Alex hovered in the background and did not seem too bothered about what he had done to me. Atarah stood by his side. She was more concerned than he was and she was angry with him and made sure he knew it.

"How could you be so stupid?" she hissed at him. "Now you could ruin everything and all for the sake of your own bruised ego."

Alex remained silent. He just stood and watched as I was put back together.

"She may die because of your resentment towards your father. She still heals like a human. She's not like us. She can't heal as we do!" She raised her voice.

As my still body was gently turned around onto my back, one of the medics lightly squeezed some clear fluid on my abdomen.

"What's that for?" Atarah questioned him.

"We have to determine that there is no internal bleeding. It is precautionary," he replied. She stood back again and let them carry on.

A probe, like a thick blunt pen was placed over my skin and was moved over the jelly-like lubricant. On the monitor, I could see the inside of my body. It was all black and fuzzy looking, just like the images on a television when the channel went dead. The medic that was performing the scan looked surprised and turned back toward Atarah and Alex.

"What is it? What's wrong?" she asked.

"Well, everything appears to be ok. There is no damage, no internal bleeding, but there is something you should see," he said, looking at Alex.

"What is it now?" he mumbled arrogantly as he walked over beside the bed.

"Your wife is with child, my Lord," he said, a broad smile on his face.

Alex looked stunned. "What? Show me!"

The medic slid the probe further over my abdomen and held it in place as he pointed to the screen. "You see that there? That is the beginnings of your child and there is the foetal heart beating away."

Alex was speechless. He stood by my side watching the tiny heartbeat as I lay in a dead-like state.

"And you are sure of this?" Atarah piped in. "The pregnancy is established?"

"Yes. From the size, I'd say she is seven to eight weeks."

Oh my God. Afanas was right. He knew all along that I was carrying Alex's child. All the while, I had been hoping that somehow there could have been a possibility that the child was Marc's.

Boy, was I wrong!

Bewilderment spread across Alex's face and from the look of his body language, he was scared. Atarah, on the other hand, was smiling like I had never seen before, her teeth gleaming in the bright light of the room. Her green eyes flickered as euphoria swept through her.

"I told you, Alexander. I knew she would be perfect. We will have our day." She laughed gleefully as she left the room.

"Yes, we'll have our day," Alex replied thoughtfully as he looked back at me.

I was left alone, my wounds unhealed and with the knowledge that my baby would be taken from me. I had to find the strength from somewhere. I needed to muster up some kind of courage if I was going to go to war with the Baranskis.

I had to stop them, one way or another.

* * *

As so often, I had been thrust into another situation that I thought would never happen. I honestly had not thought I would ever fall pregnant and right now, I found it hard to believe. I did not feel any different. I looked the same and the only real telltale sign was the awful sickness I was suffering that I had put down to the lack of food and life energy.

The healing process was taking its time and by now, my patience was beginning to come away at the seams. I hated lying there and having the three stooges take turns to watch over me made me feel even more a part of the ever growing freak show.

Three days passed, although I hardly realised it. I was losing time. The room was kept dark and there was not a hint of fresh air allowed in. I was a prisoner yet again.

"Can I at least have some magazines?" I complained to stooge number one.

He remained inanimate, as usual. His rough complexion and uncoordinated stagger amused me a little. He was not old, but, God, he had seen better days.

"So are you a vampire, as well?" I blurted out.

Again, he said nothing and for what seemed like the first time in ages, I thought about being a bitch. At least bitches get their way, or so I thought.

"So, I guess you are one of them. You all look the same, anyway. Pale, ugly, and dead. You don't say much do you?" I said as I began to laugh. "Oh, I get it. Alex got to you, too. Except, he cut out your tongue and made you a mute bastard."

It hurt to laugh, but damn, it felt good. I could not remember a time in the past three months when I had let go of all my aggression. I was done being uptight, because it seriously gets you nowhere.

"Enough!" came a voice I had not heard from since before I was taken.

Leonid.

"Sergei, you may leave," he said as he pulled up a chair beside the bed. "You can cut the smart ass attitude. It really doesn't suit you. Now explain."

His face was the usual gorgeousness, but his eyes told a different story. He was pissed at me and I knew full well how angry he could get.

"After I . . . killed Nikita . . . I ran and didn't stop. They were waiting for me and they took me to some God awful place." I held back my tears, refusing to allow my emotions cloud my clarity.

"Who waited for you?"

"The shadows. They knew where I was and they will come for me again. I can feel it."

He pondered that for a few minutes before speaking again. "How has Alex taken the news of the child?"

"Oh, you know?" I asked him, surprised that the news had reached him so fast.

"It is common knowledge now," he calmly replied.

"I'm sorry. I didn't know," I cried, shaking my head.

"I know."

He got up from the chair and sat on the bed beside me. Taking my hand in his, he whispered, "There is still a chance that the child can be brought up in the light. He doesn't have to embrace the darkness. I meant it when I said that you were mine now. Although our bond is no match for yours and Alexander's, I could feel something between us that hasn't happened to me for a long time. You could love me, Giselle. I can feel it."

"Leonid, I don't know how I feel about anything right now. I so wanted to believe that Alex was good, but he proved my doubts right. I can see now that he is capable of so many things and I can't take that risk with you. How can I be sure that you won't do this to me? He is, after all, your son," I said as a tear leaked from my eye.

"I would never hurt you, not like this. Yes, I'm capable of many things and I know I threatened you with your family's safety, but I am not a monster."

"Afanas was so wrong about a lot of things," I muttered.

"What has he got to do with any of this?" he asked as he rubbed the side of my right thumb.

"It was Afanas who had first summoned the shadows. He called them forth to take the child from me. They wanted to kill me and have me reborn as some dark Queen, but he has seen the error he made and I would never have escaped if it wasn't for him."

"He betrayed me? A century old friendship destroyed by treason! There will be no redemption for this."

"No! You mustn't hurt him. I trust him with my life," I shouted.

I held onto his hand and refused to let go when he tried to pull away from me. He was hurt and angry, but most of all he was resentful.

"Then more fool you," he said as he got up from beside me.

"Leonid, if you really love me, please let him live. Don't destroy him."

He left without saying anything. His company was replaced by the same mute medic who was tending to me. He approached my side and motioned for me to move forward. He changed the dressing on my back. It stung like hell and the pain left me dizzy.

I cried out as the gauze stuck to scabs that had begun to form over the deep cuts. The stitching was getting tighter and I could feel my skin start to knit together. The pain was replaced by the same nauseating feeling that came from the pit of my stomach. I retched and all the food I had consumed that morning was brought back up, undigested.

"Tell me this will stop some time soon!" I said.

"It will fade. Your body is going through many changes and you have to accept this as a way of nature taking over." He spoke as he lifted the basin of vomit from my lap.

"So you do speak?" I mocked.

"Only when I need to."

"When can I leave this room? I need air. I need my own bed."

"You can leave any time, although I doubt you will want to return to your room. It is in quite a mess at present."

"Oh! Yeah, I almost forgot. Can't you find somewhere else for me?" I pleaded with him.

"Mmm, I'll see what I can do, but you have to promise to stop fidgeting. Your wounds won't heal if you keep moving."

"Okay, it's a deal," I smiled. "Sergei?" I called after him.

"Yes?"

"I want to see Alex."

"I'll be sure to pass the message on," he said as he left the room.

I was on my own yet again, left to wallow in my own self-pity. I missed my mother so much and wished that I could share the news with her. I knew she would probably freak out at the prospect of being a grandmother, but I longed for her words of wisdom. Her usual way of making a bad situation seem okay was what I needed right then. I needed to be the child and have her mother protect her, even in these circumstances.

Sometime later, Alex came by. He looked gorgeous as usual but his demeanour left a lot to be desired. He strolled in through the door wearing a purplish blue shirt and black jeans. His hair was messy, as always, but I think he styled it that way. He swaggered over to my side and sat down on the bed beside me.

"I hear you wanted to see me," he said as he ran a hand through his hair.

I shuffled uneasily, pulling the covers tighter around my abdomen.

"Yeah . . . um . . . we need to talk, Alex."

"Then talk."

"I know you don't love me and you know I've never loved you. This baby . . . Do you even want it?"

"Well, I'm not too bothered, either way, but the child is wanted by my people, so I guess you could say that the needs far outweigh the want," he chortled.

"How can you be so cruel? This child will need love from its parents, us. Are you really just going to hand him or her over to the Nelapsi?" I asked.

"My son will not need the kind of love you wish to offer. He will have only one concern and that will be blood and power."

"I hate you. I really do. You could never be the man your father is. He will not allow this to happen."

He interrupted me. "Oh, now it's you and my father against us all? Good luck with that. I doubt you will get very far." He got up and started to leave. "And, for the record, I did love you, even though it was brief. With you, I felt something I have never experienced before. If you had not reacted the way you did, it would have grown and maybe things would have changed, but you destroyed it all. And now that you're in love with my father, there is no going back. You will serve your purpose and give birth to the child, but after that the shadows can have you. You can rot in hell for all I care."

I could not believe the things he said to me. He knew about the shadows all along and with this new knowledge, I was more determined than ever to break away from here. I just had to make sure that Leonid meant what he had said and, if it was true, then maybe we were meant to be together.

Maybe.

Chapter 20

Sergei came back and found me trying to get out of the bed. I stumbled as I battled to put my shoes on. He looked pretty pissed at me and I knew I was pushing my luck with him. After all, I had promised him that I would stay still if he got me the room I wanted.

"What is the meaning of this?" he screeched as he came over to my side and helped support me.

"I just want to be taken to Leonid. Please, I can't be left here any longer. It's not safe," I cried.

"I can't. I would be disobeying orders." His voice became a whisper.

"I promise you Leonid will protect you. Please?" I begged him. My eyes were already burning from the tears I had shed earlier, but now they stung like the wounds on my back.

"Okay, but please, do not say that I helped you or I shall be done for," he pleaded with me.

I saw the desperation in his eyes. Although they were red, I saw what was left of his humanity in them. I held his hand, squeezing tight. "I give you my word, Sergei."

He helped me out of the small room and through a long hallway that led us up some narrow winding stairs.

"Are you able to climb these?" he whispered in my ear.

I nodded, conserving my energy for the steep climb. As we proceeded up, I fought the pain that began to consume me. I could feel the burning sensation that blazed over my back as I took each step. Breathing through the pain, I whimpered as I held tight onto Sergei. He carefully helped me up each step and finally, we were at the top.

"Rest a little," he said to me.

I refused, shaking my head. "No! I want Leonid!"

We moved on, through a series of corridors that reminded me of the tunnels of the shadow world. Coming to a stop outside large double mahogany doors, Sergei knocked and as we waited, moonlight began to shine in through the two small windows in the back wall.

The doors opened. Leonid was obviously surprised, but I was pretty sure he was glad to see me. As Sergei helped me into the room, Leonid took my other arm and led me to his bed. Cautiously, the pair of them laid me down gently, aware of the pain I was in. I grimaced as my back made contact with the mattress.

"Shush, don't fight it," Leonid whispered.

Closing my eyes, I stopped fighting and tried to relax. Before Sergei left, I motioned him to me. I took his hand and begged, "Leonid, promise me you'll protect him. Do this for me . . . and . . . I'll never . . ." My words failed me as I fell into a deep sleep.

* * *

I do not know how long I had slept, but when I awoke I felt more alive than I had done for weeks. The nausea had settled and I was finally beginning to get my appetite back. The tightness of my back had loosened and I was able to stand up on my own without Leonid's help. He watched me as I took small steps towards the bathroom. I wanted to wash and get rid of the feel of blood across my skin. It made me feel dirty and reminded me of the violent attack from Alex.

"What do you think you're doing?" Leonid asked me as I began to run a bath.

"I stink and I feel disgusting. I just want to feel a little normal again," I said sadly as I poured some cream soap under the running hot water.

"Mmm, then at least let me help. You can't get the stitching wet."

I cringed at the thought of having him bathe me but, admittedly, I needed help. I still was not one hundred percent and I knew I had to swallow my pride. "Okay! But don't look! Turn your back so I can get in."

He smiled and nodded at me. He was so different and so gentle. He never once made me feel like some dumb school girl who got knocked up. I think he respected me.

I slid into the warm, soapy water and relished the feeling as the stains of blood washed off of me. He gently sponged water over the edges of my back, being careful not to wet the stitches. My hair felt awful, but because of the stitching I was unable to wash away the dried blood.

Once much of the blood had been cleaned from me, Leonid helped me to my feet and wrapped the towel around me. My stomach rumbled and I knew he could hear the loud noises of hunger. Flustered, I cringed.

"Are you hungry?" he asked me.

"Err, famished, actually."

I stood and looked at him as he smiled down at me. His fangs glistened in the bright light of the bathroom. His scent was delicious and I craved it so badly. The longer he stood there, the thirstier I became. As he moved in closer to me, his aroma grew more intense.

Instantly, a buzz of excitement ran through me. I wanted to drink from him so badly. I wanted to feel his warm blood sink into me and satisfy the burning desire. I wanted to consume every inch of him.

He pulled me gently into his arms and placed his lips on mine. The touch was like velvet. As I kissed him back, I savoured the taste of him. His breath was like a cyclone; it made my head spin in circles and the air between was hot.

Slowly, he eased away from our embrace and looked uncomfortable. I did not want him to stop. I wanted more and as I tried to resume, he rejected me and walked away from me.

A mixture of emotions ran through me. My increasing longing for him confused me. I knew it was not love, but deep down inside I wanted to be his only love. Where this was coming from I had no idea, but at that moment, I was willing to give it a try. If I could not have Marc, then at least I could have Leonid.

"What's wrong?" I asked as I followed him into the bedroom.

He looked sombre. "It would be wrong of me to take advantage of you while you are unwell."

"If I didn't want you to, don't you think I would have said something?"

"Giselle, I will not engage in any form of intimacy with you while you carry the child of my son."

I was completely taken aback, and sat on the edge of the bed. "But why? I don't understand," I whispered.

"It would be wrong."

"Oh great, a vampire with morals," I shouted.

"It would not feel right to me. Others would have no problem taking advantage of you, but I want more than others seek," he said with sorrow in his voice.

"So, you mean to tell me that you are willing to abstain from sex with me for another seven months? You're a man; you'll get it from somewhere. Guys always do. You'll return to Atarah and I'll be left alone again. You will forget about me," I shouted at him as I went into the bathroom and slammed the door shut behind me.

Several minutes passed before he spoke to me. "Atarah is no longer my concern. I am through with her. Giselle, I don't mean to reject you." His voice echoed through the door.

"Then don't. You can't make me feel like this and then do nothing."

"If truth be told, there is nothing stopping me from breaking down this door and taking you right now, but because I have certain feelings for you, I refuse to follow that primal urge." His voice was soft and broken.

I opened the door and looked into his red eyes. "What?"

"I have fallen in love with you and I would travel to the edge of the world for you."

Without a second thought, I fell into his arms and held him tight. His arms closed around me, and he held me tightly against his chest.

"I think I love you, too," I whispered.

I had actually said it. I could not believe what I was doing. Was I really falling for him and, if I was, what about Marc?

Of course, these thoughts had to be pushed to the back of my mind when Atarah walked in. She peered at me like I was nothing and I could see the hate in her eyes. She was evil and she was wearing it well today.

"Getting rather cosy, I see," she sneered, running her long fingernails across the wall as she walked closer to us.

"What do you want, Atarah?" Leonid asked, shielding me from her gaze.

"Oh, darling Leo, you know what I want. It only happens to be in your, what should I call her, um . . . oh, yes, your little concubine." She laughed. "That child is to be mine, so don't get too comfortable, Giselle. I will take what belongs to me."

Anger welled inside me, and before Leonid could hold me back I was in front of her, staring hard into the beautiful, cold face of hers. "You will never take my baby from me. I will see you dead before my child is corrupted by you or Alex. I swear to you now, if you come anywhere near me again I'll rip your frigging throat out. You're nothing but a barren, self righteous bitch."

Her eyes widened, but before she could strike me, Leonid caught her arm and pushed her back towards the door. "For over a century I sat back and allowed you your freedom. I gave you everything you ever needed, and for what? To have you scheme behind my back and corrupt the mind of my only child. I have awoken to your treachery and now, I fear, there is no redemption for you. I can assure you now that, given time, I will repay you all the wrongs you have done. Now, leave."

Standing in astonishment, I watched the power surge out from Leonid as he all but carried her out of the room.

"You do not scare me. Remember, I know you, Leo. I know all your little tricks. I just hope you're ready for what is coming," she screeched from the corridor. "Mark my words, I will have that child!"

Her voice echoed in my head as I began to realise the seriousness of what was happening. "Oh my God, they're going to do it, aren't they?" I panicked. "They're going to take my baby."

"Giselle, I will not let anything happen to you or your child," he said confidently.

"How can you be so sure?"

"Because I will kill them."

Leonid meant what he said. I could see it in his face. He was angry and Atarah had aggravated him by threatening me. I knew that look he wore upon his face. He was planning something.

"We must leave at once," he said. "Get dressed. I will be back shortly."

He left the room before I had the chance to say anything else. I knew I was healing, but I was not so sure about traveling again and I certainly did not want to go back to the Kerguelen Islands.

My stomach churned as waves of heat and dizziness overcame me. I had thought they were long gone and now the nausea depleted me of the energy I had conserved. I vomited into the waste bin and continued until it felt as though the lining of my stomach had all but been removed. I sat back against the wooden paneled wall and waited for the moment to pass.

Gradually, the room stopped spinning and the heat that had overcome me began to die, leaving my skin clammy and sticky. I hesitated to move at first, wary of the sickly feeling taking over again, but in spite of myself I got to my feet and carefully pulled on a pair of black jeans and cautiously pulled a pink jumper over my head, trying my best not to let the material rub against the stitching. It hurt, but was bearable.

By the time I had dressed myself and fixed my hair into a loose braid, Leonid had returned along with Antoine who always seemed to turn up whenever there was a crisis. He seemed his usual jovial self, but I could see the worry on his face. They both exchanged a wary look and I knew that things were getting serious.

"Okay . . . What's going on?" I asked, folding my arms.

"Whatever could be wrong, sweet Princess? You have two fine men at your disposal and if something were to arise, believe me, we are more than ready for action," Antoine remarked as he peered out of the window.

"Bylun is waiting and I assured him we wouldn't be long," Leonid said as he helped me to my feet, not that I needed help. After all, I had successfully dressed myself on my own.

"Has something happened?"

"Giselle, we must leave now," Leonid beckoned.

"Not until you tell me why."

"Now is not the time for stubbornness. We have minutes before they come," he said as he coaxed me towards the door.

"Who's coming? Leonid, who is coming?" I begged him.

"The gluttons. The Nelapsi young."

The name resonated through my head. Alex had told me about them when I had first came to Armenia, but something about the name and the reactions in both Leonid and Antoine sent warning signals rushing to my brain. I knew then that things were going to get bad, real bad.

Chapter 21

We rushed through blacked out tunnels where I could hear the sounds of dripping water and the rush of tiny feet beneath me. My hand remained firmly in Leonid's as he led the way. Behind me, Antoine followed, steadying me whenever my feet let me down. Neither of them spoke and because of the seriousness of the situation, I refused to utter a word. I was frightened for myself and for my unborn child.

We came to a stop in the darkness and, all of a sudden, a ball of light hurt the back of my eyes, making me squint. Antoine held out his hand and in his palm sat a small, round ball. Its flame had a subtle orange glow and gave me enough light to see the steel door in front of us.

"Where are we?" I whispered.

"At the foothills of the mountain," Leonid answered as he pushed hard against the door.

"Bylun is on the other side waiting for us," Antoine spoke casually as he held the flame up closer to me.

"How?" I asked, pointing at his hand.

"We all have our own party tricks. This is mine." He smiled.

From behind came a loud crash. All three of us looked back down in the direction of the long line of blackness. In the distance came the sounds of rushed feet, accompanied by the noises of inhumane squeals. High-pitched shouts and laughter echoed around us and the hairs on my skin stood on end. I was so frightened and I did not know if there was any chance of escape.

Leonid pushed harder to no effect. Gritting his teeth, he heaved against the door and finally, it edged open and light came streaming in. I was pushed through the doorway to be met by the white bearded man who had helped me before. His smile was a welcome sight and taking me by the hand, he hugged me tight.

Bylun.

Behind me, I could hear a scuffle. Screams and shouts, and bloodcurdling noises came from the direction of the tunnel. Antoine shouted something at me, but because of the noise I could not make out what he had said. I soon realised that Leonid was nowhere to be seen. I knew he had been right by my side when I left the tunnel, but now he was gone.

Antoine shouted at me again, but still I did not hear what he said. I was more concerned about Leonid. I moved back towards the door. Bylun tried to stop me, but failed. I moved closer and was instantly hit with the smell of blood. It did not smell good. I could sense so much death around me and something told me I was walking back into a trap. Even so, I was determined to find out what was going on.

I could make out Leonid as he fought three vampires who all resembled Afanas. Their eyes glowed red in the darkened tunnel. They screeched and hissed as they drew their claws out, cutting and slicing at Leonid who seemed invincible. He towered over them, ripping them in half.

From behind, came another two with weapons in their hands. One had what looked like a pickaxe, while the other held a spear as they attacked Leonid. Antoine came charging at them, biting clean through the neck of one of them as his axe fell to the ground. I could hear his life hiss out of him as he choked on his own blood.

Leonid moved with a speed that I found hard to believe was possible. He seemed so powerful and in control of the situation that I did not understand what was happening when I saw the spear appear through his chest. He stopped moving and looked down at the head of the spear drenched in blood. Looking back at me, his eyes filled with bloody tears and silently, he fell to the ground.

Laughing and screaming, the rogue vampire ran back down the dark tunnel. Red, blazing eyes met me as I walked in further. His mouth dripped with blood.

"Don't!" Antoine grabbed hold of my wrist.

Confused, I pushed past him and went further down into the tunnel, making my way over to Leonid. The smell intensified as I came closer him

"Leo . . ." I began, my voice shaking.

"Giselle, please, don't come any closer," he said, his breathing laboured.

"No. No, Leonid . . ." I cried as I approached him as he lay upon the wet ground.

His hand covered his chest and I could clearly see the line of crimson spreading rapidly through his fingers. His neck had been wounded and the blood flowed beneath him.

Rushing to his side, I rubbed his face as his eyes met mine. He looked at me so lovingl, and the memory of the man I had first met died and was replaced by the memories of the man who adored me and loved me. Our union was not ideal, but somehow, through all the chaos, I had found my broken heart mended. He had, in his own way, made me fall in love with him and now I was not ready to let go of that.

"You're not going anywhere. Do you hear me?" I shouted through sobs.

He tried to speak, but he was losing too much blood. "Shush, don't talk. Save your strength," I whispered as I put my hand over his.

Antoine stood behind us. He lit up the area around us, and it was then I saw the corpses lying around us. More than twenty vampires lay dead, their heads severed from their bodies. I looked back at Antoine who stood looking sad.

"What happened?" I asked.

"There were too many. He could only take on so many. You saw the one who got away."

"What are they?"

"The young of the Nelapsi. They sent their young to kill him. Without him by your side, you are defenceless. He's fatally wounded, Giselle. There is no way to save him."

"But we've got to try!" I cried.

"It would be pointless," Antoine tried to reason with me.

My skin crawled yet again as my stomach turned. Leonid gasped and reached out his hand to my face. I did not want to believe that I was about to lose him just when I had found him. There had to be a way to save him.

"I cannot remember a time . . . when . . ." he struggled. "When I felt whole, like I do now. Giselle, I have never loved anyone the way that I love you." He paused as he tried to regain his breath.

"Don't . . . please . . . please . . ." I begged him.

"You . . . you have no idea how special you are," He coughed up blood. "I know that you could never love me the way I love you, but promise me this. Do not let them near the child and learn to love another."

"I do . . . I do love you, you stupid man. Please . . . don't go," I sobbed, holding his hand to my face. Afraid to let go, I tightened my grip.

Slowly, his hand loosened its hold on my face. His eyes became vacant and held their gaze on me. I watched him, holding my breath as his breathing became shallow and with one last kiss upon his lips, he stopped breathing altogether. I cried as I threw myself onto him.

"You promised! You promised you wouldn't leave me. Please, just . . . just stay. Stay with me, please, Leonid. Don't leave me!" I broke down, crying over his still body.

Antoine placed his hands on my shoulder and tried to lift me from Leonid. "He's gone, Giselle. He's dead."

I sat beside the still, lifeless body of the only man who was willing to die for me. My heart ached for him and as I willed him to live on, I knew deep down inside that he was never coming back. Perhaps, in time, that would be something I would learn to accept, but right there and then, I wanted to die with him.

I did not have the fight or the courage to carry on without him. Perhaps it was selfish, but to have been killed along with him felt as though it would have been better than to grieve over the loss of someone so special.

Antoine knelt down beside me and tried to persuade me to move from Leonid's side, but nothing was going to make me leave him there. I wanted to take his body with me. I wanted to give him a proper send off even he would have been proud of.

"Sweet, sweet, Princess . . . Please, we must go."

"No!" I shouted. "I can't leave him here. I won't!"

"But they'll be back. They will come down here, and when they find you . . . well, let's just say you will never see daylight again."

"Antoine, please! Look at him. We can't leave him like this. Surely, we can do something? Bylun! He can do his . . .

you know, thingy. At least, that way we can bury him or whatever you do when a vampire dies."

"I'm not sure Bylun would be able to do it," Antoine said softly.

"Please, Antoine. At least try!" I begged.

Antoine got up from behind me and walked to the doorway where Bylun stood sombrely. The pair of them spoke together quietly. I was unable to make out what they were saying. Finally, Bylun nodded and Antoine returned to my side.

"Giselle! It is time. With Bylun's help, we will bring the body of His Highness with us."

I was unable to speak. Instead, my sobs echoed through the darkness as Antoine lifted Leonid into his arms and carried him out of the darkness and into the light. Bylun waited for me at the doorway and I broken-heartedly walked towards him. As he took me by the hand, I felt his power surge into me. Even though it was brief, it gave me enough energy to carry on.

Outside, the bright light of the sun shone down on us as we made our way from the tunnel. Antoine laid Leonid on the soft mossy grass. Red, pink, blue, yellow, and purple flowers were strewn across the meadow as though an ocean wave had tossed them there, but it was Leonid's blood that tarnished the beautiful valley around us.

The alpine meadow teeming with wild flowers no longer appealed to me. They now reminded me of death. When I knelt down beside him, Bylun recited something and with one stroke of his staff against the ground, a ball of blazing light surrounded us and felt as if we were floating through the air. Everything became a blur.

My body seemed to have disintegrated into tiny particles. Warmth enveloped me as I spun in the air. Shimmering light cascaded all around me, like nothing I had ever seen or experienced before. I felt completely at peace, even though it lasted only seconds.

With a sudden jerk, I was whole again. I was close to Leonid's body, only now my surroundings were very different. Leonid lay on a stone table in the centre of a small room. All around us, white symbols were painted on the walls and candles burned brightly in each corner. I looked around trying to see a door, and found nothing.

Three more men appeared out of nowhere, each one resembling Bylun but different in his own way. The smallest of the three had a shorter white beard and carried in his hands a small wooden box. The next man had long grey hair and in his hand, he held a large, brown, leather bound book. The last of them stood closest to Bylun and although they seemed the same, this man had one black eye that looked like a marble.

Each one took a place at the corner of the table. Bylun had a grim look on his face and as he began to speak, my feet gave way and I found myself lying on the ground, shaking uncontrollably. Everything that I loved or cared about was being taken from me and there was nothing I could do to change that.

Chapter 22

The cold realisation began to hit me and I was petrified at the thought that I would never see Leonid again. I was not ready to let go. I did not want to. Antoine, as usual, tended to me and helped me to my feet. I stood at the wall and pressed my back up against the coldness.

Antoine did not leave my side for a moment.

"Take this man. Take him now forever to face the other world. By the earth, wind, fire, and rain, send him on his way. Remember him. Take him, embrace him, and release him from his binds," Bylun recited as he moved round the table holding incense in his hand and shaking it over Leonid's body.

The smell burned the back of my nose as the increasing smoke settled on Leonid. The three men began to undress Leonid and realising what was happening, I ran over to them, shouting.

"Get away from him! Do not touch him again."

"Giselle, we must prepare the body for burial," Bylun said gently.

"No! Leave him as he is."

"We cannot send him into the other world unless he has been cleansed. Surely, you can understand that much. His Goddess will not accept him unless it is done."

I looked over my shoulder at Antoine, who remained settled against the wall. "He's right, but if you believe he can pass on without this, then so be it." He shrugged his shoulders.

"I . . . I can't watch this." I looked away as I walked and faced the wall. "Take me from here, please!" I begged.

"Close your eyes," Antoine said.

I looked at him, confused. "What?"

"Just do it."

I closed my eyes tightly and tried to rid my mind of all the pain and anguish that continued to build up. I felt Antoine's hand in mine and feeling a sudden rush of heat, I slowly opened my eyes. I saw that we were no longer in the room, but on the top of what looked like a turret on the tower of a castle. Wind blew my braid loose and as I looked over the edge, I saw waves crashing hard against the rocks below.

I looked out over the vast horizon and saw that there was no other land around us. It was as if we were the only people that existed here. It was an amazing sight and my heart skipped a beat as I watched the waves violently burst their froth over the pointed and rugged rocks that sat beneath the ivory stone building.

"Why does this keep happening to me? It's so unfair," I asked as I leaned further over the edge of the turret, imagining what it would feel like to fall into the waves below.

"I wish I had the answers you seek, but I'm afraid I'm as ignorant as you. Maybe it's the Goddess's way of testing you."

"Antoine, how am I meant to do this without him? He saved me from them more than once and now I have no one. I am totally alone again."

"But you seemed to have overlooked one thing."

"Yeah, what's that?" I asked.

"Me! You have me, Giselle. I am not going anywhere." His voice was so soft and I knew he meant what he said although I did not believe him. I knew that Atarah and Alex would somehow eventually get to him and I did not want to be responsible for his death as well.

"Antoine, I think it would be better if you were to . . . I don't know – forget about me. I know they'll try to get to me through you and I can't have that on my conscience. If I'm to have this baby, then I'll do it alone." I walked away from him.

"Sorry you feel that way, but the way I see it you don't have much of a choice in the matter. I'm staying, so get used to having me and my rugged good looks around."

Sometimes, he infuriated me to the point were I wanted to punch the crap out of him. Other times, I wanted to hug him. He had a funny way of showing it, but I was pretty sure he cared about me.

"But what happens if they come? Leo . . ." My voice broke. "He thought he could protect me and look what happened to him."

"Leonid was blindsided by his love for you. He underestimated Atarah."

"He didn't know she'd send the Nelapsi after me?"

"Of course, he did. He just didn't expect so many of their young in the tunnel. He fought like a true warrior and even as he died, he was relentless. Now, stop blaming yourself and think of the one person we all need to protect. Your unborn child needs nourishment and sustenance and our standing here debating who we should blame for Leonid's death will not accomplish anything."

"But . . ."

He cut me off. "Take my hand," he commanded. "It is time."

And, like a child, I held on tight.

* * *

The fire blazed as it spat bright colours of orange and yellow out amongst the burning embers. Its heat radiated the area around us and as I watched Leonid's body burning, I felt a piece of my heart dying as he slowly perished under the tremendous heat. I watched in silence, unable to cry. My sudden loss of emotions came as relief to me. I felt numb and accepted that I would feel like this for some time.

Bylun stood close to the other three lesser Gods as they, too, looked on earnestly. I saw grief in their eyes and this was something I thought would never be possible. Considering what Leonid had been, it was hard to imagine a source of goodness feeling anything other than contempt for a vampire.

Leonid's death had clearly moved them, just as it had affected Antoine. He stood back on his own. His eyes had glazed over and through the reflection of the flames in his eyes, I saw tears. I knew that they had been close, but I had not known enough about their relationship to make any kind of presumptions. I was moved by his demeanour and I knew that he, too, had been changed by what was happening.

Slowly, the fire consumed what was left of Leonid. He was now nothing more than ash in the late evening sun. Moments later, I was left alone as Bylun and Atone retreated back inside the medieval looking castle. Walking up to the remains of the fire, I watched as a gentle breeze carried the ash into the air, spreading it out across the water below.

From inside me, I could feel anger swell. I could not understand why this was happening to me. I had always thought I was a good person. I had never done any wrong to anyone and now in such a short period of time, my life had fallen apart.

"Why me? Why couldn't you have chosen somebody else?" I shouted into the sky as the sun began to set.

From out of nowhere, a white light appeared before me hovering in the air. It hurt my eyes to look at it, but through my fingers I could make out the silhouette of a man. He drifted closer to me and became more and more recognizable.

"How?" I asked as I began to shake.

"Do not be frightened. I have a message for you from the Goddess," he spoke.

I shook my head in disbelief at what I was seeing. "No! I am seriously out of it right now. This cannot be happening."

"It can and it is. Giselle, look at me," he asked.

I stared hard at my feet, trying my best to refuse to believe what I was seeing.

"Very well, then. I come with news of the unborn."

Now I looked up at him. His face was exactly the same. He was how I would always remember him, strong, beautiful, and completely in love with me.

"What about the baby?" I asked him.

"Your child is destined for great things, but, as with all journeys, yours has only just begun. You have many hurdles to cross and given time, you will learn to accept your fate. Do not trust those who insist that they have your best interests at heart, for it is they who will push the dagger in deeper."

He began to fade into the evening sky and my heart started to crumble. I felt as though I was losing him all over again.

"Leonid!" I yelled his name. "Please . . . don't go." My voice was failing me and just when I had thought I had heard the last of him, his voice came to me through a gust of wind.

"Giselle, you will learn to love again. Trust your heart as you did me. Farewell, my love."

And then he was gone.

I gripped tightly onto the stone wall and anxiously waited for him to return, but he never did. Inside, I fell to pieces as I began to realise that I would never ever see Leonid again. Instead of crying like any normal person, I roared out loud, screaming obscenities at the sky. I was seriously pissed off and I had just about had enough of having my heart broken.

In such a short time, I had been turned into some new breed of vampire, been married, knocked up, found out my mother was seriously ill, been kidnapped by creatures of the shadow world, slept with my father-in-law, and just when I thought I had loved him, he was taken from me. Quite a heavy load to bear and I had just about had my gut full.

Pacing like a mad woman, I wanted to make Atarah and Alex pay for what they had done to me. I wanted to see them suffer the same pain I had endured and the only way I knew involved me returning to Armenia and taking action myself.

Antoine would be pretty pissed, but I did not see any other way. I waited until the sun had disappeared from the sky and watched the dark clouds consume the land around me. The only noise was from the surf lapping against the overhanging rocks below.

"I think you ought to retire." A voice came from behind me.

"Nah, I've too much on my mind," I replied.

"Sweet Princess, we both know that you have experienced a little too much. I suggest some much needed rest."

"Oh, cut the bullshit, Antoine!" I barked back at him.

"Not the language you'd expect from a Princess. But under the circumstances, I dare say that things have taken their toll on you. Please, Giselle, rest a little. If not for you, then for the child."

I shuffled my feet as I struggled to ignore him. He, like Alex, had a way of making me succumb to his way of thinking. I looked at him and his perfectly formed face and I hated to admit it, but he had won. It was pointless trying to argue with him and I accepted defeat.

"Okay. But only for the sake of the baby," I said as I walked towards a wooden door.

"Of course. Only for the sake of the child," he agreed as he raised an eyebrow, chuckling to himself.

I refused to be something that was self destructive and my main driving force was now my unborn child. I had a responsibility that concerned more than me. For once in my life, I was willing to think of someone other than myself.

This time I was not scared. It was as though I had woken up from a bad dream. All I needed to do was to place my trust in Antoine and somehow, together, we would defeat the Nelapsi. From where I stood, it was going to be a simple battle. There could only be one victor and I was determined that it would be me.

I was led into a small, quirky room that reminded me of my best friend Erin's room back home. Bold colours of green and purple covered the walls and neatly tucked away in the corner was a small bed. Admittedly, it was a welcome sight and my now exhausted body craved the warmth and comfort of a pillow and blanket. I think Antoine was pretty convinced that I would rest as I had said I would and without a fight, I lay down and closed my eyes.

My sleep was sound and undisturbed by dreams. The only thing that hurt was waking and knowing that it would be Antoine greeting me and not the greenish red eyes of Leonid. My heart sank to new depths.

I tried to ignore the growing feeling of the presence of someone in the room with me. He stood in the corner watching me, observing my thoughts, and with a little more fight in me than I had expected, I shouted out at the dark shadow.

"For Pete's sake, can't I even think in peace any more?"

"I just wanted to make sure that there would be no repeat of the little episode that involved you hanging out of windows," Antoine joked sarcastically.

"That's not funny you know!" I lowered my voice.

"No. It wasn't. Yet I have my suspicions. Remember, I know you, sweet Princess. I can tell when you aren't exactly yourself."

"Oh, come off it. When have I ever been myself around you?"

"I can think of a few times, but I we can save those for a time when 'life' isn't so precarious."

Scoffing, I pulled the blanket off of my legs. That was when the usual nausea overcame me and, without much of a warning for Antoine, I vomited on the ground. I retched as I held back tears. I was embarrassed that he had witnessed me at my worst, but also relieved that I had not choked to death on the amount of liquid that came up.

As I wiped my hand across my mouth, Antoine handed me his handkerchief. I looked up at him and accepted it, using it to remove the residue from my chin.

"Thanks," I muttered.

"Are you okay?" he asked me, concerned.

"Yep! It'll pass. It normally does."

"Right, then I guess we'd best hurry. Bylun is sending us on a little trip," he exclaimed gleefully.

"What?"

"Mmm, a little round trip that should last around seven months or so."

"Antoine, stop talking in riddles." I began to get mad at him.

"We're going to secure you and the child, one way or another. And, of course, the only way to do that is to make you disappear off the planet altogether."

"I don't like the sound of this," I said cautiously.

"Don't be such a wimp. We'll have a blast. Now come. Let's get all the intel and make haste." He held out his beautiful hand to me and like before, I took it. He held onto me tightly as we left the room and walked towards the rest of our lives. Or, at least, the next seven months of it.

Or so I thought.

Chapter 23

Okay. Some things happen for a reason. Others happen because of circumstance, but with me, it was a case of being god-damned unlucky. I had finally accepted the path my life had taken and was preparing myself for the changes that would begin to take place within my own body, although nothing could prepare me for what I was going to go through during that process.

Antoine was in his typical hyper mood. It seemed as though nothing affected him, or so I thought. I had not given him or his feelings much thought and after what had happened to Leonid, I really was not bothered.

As we approached a long, narrow hallway, it was hard to ignore the bizarre illustrations that were displayed upon the wall. Stars and circles and odd sentences had been drawn in white along the whole length of the hall.

"What is this place?" I whispered.

"This, my sweet Princess, is the portal to another dimension," he casually replied.

"What? Seriously? Like, for real?" I was slightly tongue-tied.

We reached the door and as we entered the round room, the strangest feeling came over me. The numbness had gone and in its place, a sensation that I had never felt before rippled though me. My hands and arms tingled as if tiny needles were compressing my skin. The more intense it became, the more I liked the feeling. I felt completely out of it, as if I was high.

I could sense Antoine's glare as I smiled to myself, intoxicated by the unknown substance that was penetrating through me. He looked on, amused by my foolish behaviour and, unlike him, I lost control of my senses. I burst into a fit of giggles as I sat in the centre of the room. It spun as I tried my best to sit up straight, but the more I tried, the more I slipped to the side. I was almost wetting myself with laughter and then everything came to a stop. I immediately sobered, embarrassed by my behaviour.

I got to my feet, trying my best not to fall. The spinning sensation was still lingering in my head and if it had not been for Antoine's quick movement to my side, I think I would have fallen on my face.

"Thanks," I muttered timidly as I let him take a hold of my arm.

"That was quite a performance," he joked.

In the spirit of things, I thumped him hard on the arm. "Don't dare say another word. Got it?" I scowled.

Laughing, he led me out through the same door. Only, we did not enter the hallway. This time, the doorway led into a busy street. People rushed past us, some with bags of shopping and others on their cell phones. We passed a group of school children following their teacher. Each child held onto the hand of another and not once, did any of them look at us. They were quiet and obedient, very unlike the children back at home. We came to a little side street and instantly, the smell of fresh coffee hit me. My stomach rumbled and I craved the taste of caffeine, or food of any sort.

"Can I?" I asked.

He looked a bit annoyed, at first, but he soon smiled at me. "Who am I to deny a beautiful woman her caffeine rush, or whatever else takes her fancy?"

I glanced scornfully at him and entered the small cafe. I sat at a table far from the window and picked up the menu.

"It's all gibberish," I remarked.

"It may be gibberish to you, but here it's the norm."

On a closer inspection, I noticed that the words were spelt backwards. Even numbers were the wrong way round.

"Why?"

"Because we're on the other side of the looking glass, so to speak," he said as he riffled through his pockets.

"What's wrong?" I asked him.

"Mmm, nothing," he replied as he opened his wallet. "I knew I always carried a little extra."

"Extra what?"

"These!" He held out what looked to be dollar bills, except that they were exactly like the menu, backwards. "Can't get much without these little babies."

"Oh! Okay . . . Then I'll have a cheeseburger, fries, strawberry milkshake, and . . . onion rings. I love onion rings," I gushed.

A short, overweight woman came over and looked us up and down. "So, what can I get ya'll?" she slurred with a southern drawl.

"I'll have a coffee and the lady here will have . . ."

I butted in and placed my order with urgency. My mouth watered at the thought of the food. It seemed ages since I had last eaten and I was more than ready to fill my stomach with cholesterol-laden goodies.

"So, why this place. How can I be safe here?" I asked as I sipped over the creamy milkshake.

"Because here we remain unseen. They cannot sense you here."

"That's what you said about the Kerguelen Islands," I whispered as a man sitting at the counter looked over at us.

"Ah, but it was the shadows that found you, not Alex."

"Yeah, but . . . but can't they, like, you know, see us? Surely, they have their own kind here."

I watched eagerly as the waitress came over to us and set my food in front of me. I took the burger in my hands and bit down into the meat, savouring the taste of the well-cooked beef, creamy cheese, onions, and tomato sauce. I grabbed a handful of fries and stuffed them into my mouth and then gulped down the last of the milkshake.

"You really are hungry, aren't you?" Antoine said as he sipped some of his coffee.

"Well, I am technically eating for two now. Can't see the problem with having a few extra calories," I said as I chewed on an onion ring.

I finished the burger in less than three bites. I cannot remember having ever eaten anything so fast before in my life and now I knew why. A sudden urge to belch came over me and trying my best to conceal the build up, I held a napkin over my mouth as I hiccupped.

Antoine watched me as I uncomfortably shuffled in my seat. He was demurely sipping some more from his cup when his eyes moved in the direction of the door. I followed his gaze and I was surprised when in walked a middle-aged man. He looked so familiar, as though I had seen him somewhere before, yet he looked past me and gestured to the man at the counter.

"I think we should finish up here," Antoine said as he tossed two twenty bills on our table.

"But I'm not finished," I complained.

"Yes, you are. Come on," he said as he got up from his chair.

He stood in front of me, eyeballing me as if I was a bad child. "Please, trust me. Okay?" he said softly.

Getting up from my seat, I turned round to walk to the door and found the man who had been sitting at the counter now standing in front of me. He was big and broad and he had a hardened face. He looked down at me and smirked.

"We've been waiting for you, Miss Bergman."

Before I could respond, Antoine moved in front of me and held out his hand. "I am Antoine Vilniv. I am the Princess's keeper."

"Well, Mr. Vilniv, if you and the Princess would follow me, I'm sure we can come to some kind of understanding," the man said confidently.

"What?" I yelled, making a few of the other customers turn their attention to us.

"Giselle, not here," Antoine whispered in my ear.

Biting my lip, I listened to Antoine. Something in his voice told me that this was serious and we were about to find out just how bad things were getting. We moved outside the little cafe and were led to an awaiting black car. We both sat silently as the car moved off. I was afraid to speak in case I said the wrong thing. Antoine, on the other hand, sat back smirking at the man sitting directly in front of us.

"What?" the man asked.

"Nothing," Antoine replied, shaking his head.

Laughing out loud, he nudged me in the ribs. I looked at him, confused. For a moment, I thought he had gone mad.

"Don't piss me off, Mr. Vilniv," the man shouted.

"Excuse my behaviour. I just find this whole thing quite amusing."

"How so?" the man asked as he folded his arms.

"Well, we were granted refuge in your world, but now you have sought us out and taken us hostage." Antoine folded his arms and stared hard at the man.

"I am not at liberty to discuss this. It is not my place."

"Then who does have the authority?" Antoine asked.

The man remained silent and broke his gaze from us. Instead, he opened up his briefcase and took out a book, *To Kill A Mockingbird*. It was obviously spelt backwards.

"I did that last semester. It's good," I said, waiting for some kind of reply.

He said nothing, only glanced at me over his glasses and then returned his gaze to the book. Antoine looked at me with his perfect blue eyes, but they startled me when they flashed red. I knew something was going on inside him and with a sense of what was to happen, I tried to change his mind by diverting his attention. I grabbed his right hand and slid my fingers over his and I tightened my grip.

Shaking my head, "Please don't," I begged.

His smiled broadened and without a warning, he leaned forward and grabbed the man by the throat. He struggled to breath and spit flew out from his mouth.

"Now, before I rip your throat out and drink you dry, you will tell me who summoned us," he hissed as his fangs gleamed.

Loosening his grip on the man's throat, he smiled. "Will you behave if I let you go?" Antoine asked.

The man nodded. Breathing hard, he muttered something.

"I can't hear you. Speak up!"

"Xavier Ordina," the man said breathlessly.

I sat upright and froze. I knew that name and remembered when I had first met him. Screaming, I tried to break free from the car, only to be pulled back by Antoine.

"No! We have to leave now," I cried.

"Giselle! We must face this," Antoine told me calmly.

"No . . . You can, but I can't. He wants to kill me. He wants my baby."

Chapter 24

I hid my face in my hands and tried to regain some kind of sense of what was happening. I thought I would be safe here, but now everything seemed to be slipping away from me again. I had no control and needed to regain some measure of it. This was my life, my destiny, and I was the one who had to change the course of action.

Antoine kept his sharp gaze on the man as I kept mine on him. He looked menacing and it was the first time I had ever seen him allow the monster within him to surface. I had all but forgotten that he was a vampire. He had never once allowed me to see him in his true form and it was all too easy to think of him as human. I was stiff in the back of the car, afraid to move, but also wary of the thirst that was obvious in his eyes. I could sense his eagerness to kill the man and as much as I disliked him, I did not want to see any more unnecessary blood loss.

The car braked hard as it swerved round a bend in the road. I was thrown forward and before I hit the seat in front of me, Antoine grabbed me by my hair and pulled me back to him. It hurt like hell, but it was bearable, considering my face could have been crushed.

My heart raced as I realised that there was something happening outside. Raised voices sounded muffled from inside the car, so Antoine jerked his head towards the window and listened intently. His eyes narrowed. Something he heard caused him concern, because in the next moment, he pulled the man towards him and bit down on his neck. Hearing his fangs pierce the skin made my flesh crawl. I had never expected him to turn so quickly and hearing him swallow hard on the fresh blood brought the situation closer to home.

The man let out a small cry as Antoine drank from him. I watched, speechless, as he drank every last drop of blood, and for the third time in my life, I witnessed the death of someone at the hands of a vampire. The man's eyes glazed over as he took his last breath. His face was pale and fright shadowed around his eyes and then, finally, death came.

Antoine loosened his grip and the man fell lifeless into a heap on the seat. Antoine wiped the remains of blood from his chin and smiled at me. I was too stunned to say anything. I just looked at him open mouthed.

"This has all been a trap. Outside this car there is an ambush. They are waiting for us to run and they plan to separate us. I'm disposable. You, on the other hand, are, as Afanas so kindly put it, 'a precious commodity.' They will kill me to get to you and like a fool, I'd die for you," he said as he looked out the window, assessing the situation.

"How?" I asked.

"We obviously have an informer in our midst, but that is not our concern now. Right now, we need to escape. We have no choice. We must run for it," he said as he reached down toward the body of the man and searched him. Pulling out a gun, he smiled and slipped it into the back of his jeans and pulled lightly on the door handle.

"Now, when I say run, you run straight ahead. You don't stop. You keep going. Don't look back, okay? Never look back," he ordered.

"But . . . I'm scared," I choked.

"Now is not the time for cowardice. Giselle, do you trust me?" he asked, taking my hand in his.

"Well, yeah."

"Then do as I say."

"Okay."

The next few moments went by in what seemed like slow motion. We slipped out of the right passenger door and stayed close to it. Antoine closed it quietly as I held my breath.

We remained silent, listening to the chatter of the men on the other side of the road. The driver of our car was standing over at a checkpoint, smoking a cigarette and talking into his cell phone. He never once looked over towards us. He was too engrossed in his conversation to notice me peeking out at him from the front bumper of the car.

Feeling Antoine's hand on my right shoulder, I looked back at him as he placed a finger over my lips. I saw something in his eyes. It was not fear. It was something else and it was almost as if he was getting a kick out of the dangerous situation we were in. I wanted to believe that he was invincible, but I knew only too well how fragile vampires were. I feared for him and his life, as well as my own. I could not lose him as well.

"Whatever happens, we're in this together, right?" I whispered.

"I've made an oath to protect you and I will keep my word." He smiled at me.

"Good. Then let's do this. Not that I'm ready, but . . . Yeah . . . Let's do this," I said.

As soon as I made that affirmation, Antoine grabbed me by the hand and led me toward the back of the car. We had parked close to a grass verge on the side of a hill. Below the masses of rocks and boulders was a river and, on closer inspection, it seemed like a very long way down. I did not want to risk being killed in a fall, but the odds were against us. It was either downhill or back to the now growing convoy of cars.

Antoine pointed in the direction of the slipway and like animals, we crawled towards it. Silently, the pair of us moved across the tarmac that stopped inches from the grass. He gently pushed me over the edge and followed, keeping a firm look out. To the far left, a black hummer approached and the many men who had been standing around soon stood to attention.

The vehicle came to a stop on the other side of the checkpoint. Its doors opened and two larger-than-life men got out. They both scanned the area before one of them moved back to the vehicle and opened the rear passenger door. I could not believe my eyes when out stepped the same hunched-over silhouette I had seen when I had been taken to the Shadow World.

Xavier.

Holy shit! He had been behind this whole kidnap thing. I knew it when I heard his name from the man in the car and seeing him here brought it home to me. I really had to get away from here.

Xavier pointed to the direction of the car and panic set in. I knew it would be only minutes before they realised that I had gone and then the hunt would be on. This was not how I had imagined my place of sanctuary to be, but then again, when all things were considered, it made a change from running from Alex and Atarah.

Antoine held me close to him as he shielded me from view. I lowered myself further down the face of the embankment and finally began the decent down to the riverbank. I did not look up once. I kept on moving, concentrating on my footing, making sure I made no noise.

Not too far behind me, Antoine lowered himself down. His movements and his control was much more elegant than mine and he seemed to make effortless progress, whereas I stumbled and cut myself more often than actually accomplishing anything.

As we approached the lower end of the embankment, I heard yells, confused shouting, and then all hell broke loose. From the ridge of the slipway, two men looked down at us and pointed. They watched as I finally made solid ground and hid behind a thorn bush. Antoine, on the other hand, stood up and bowed like some actor at the end of a theatrical performance. He turned and smiled at me, winking as he pulled out the gun and fired a shot into the air.

"Jesus, are you like frigging crazy?" I yelled at him as I tried to shelter myself from the now growing audience.

"What's life without a little entertainment?" he asked as he brushed grass and grit from his clothes.

"Err, I think I'd prefer something a little low key for once."

"Yes, I'm sure you would, but, dear little Giselle, I'm not one for sitting in and reading, although I do find that entertaining. However, as you can see . . ." He pointed to the men clambering downhill, heading straight for me. "I thrive on these kinds of situations."

From both of his hands, I could see a glow building up to form full-blown balls of flames. He held them effortlessly in each hand and with a devilish twinkle in his eye, he laughed and shouted, "Showtime!" as he threw the flames at the dry grass.

Within seconds, the flames had engulfed the entire embankment. The inferno spread uphill quickly. I smiled as I watched the men retreat back up hill and found myself looking at Xavier. His face was just as I had imagined it to be. He was old and ugly and his eyes were hollow holes in his head. He was truly death himself.

I stood close to Antoine, trying to avert my gaze from the horrific apparition at the top of the embankment. "So? What now?" I asked, scratching the back of my head.

"Now, sweet Princess, we run."

Without any hesitation, I took his hand and we ran along the river bank, ducking under the overgrowth of the trees, running further and further into the dense forest as the fixed stare of Xavier's eyes faded and all that was left was Antoine, myself, and my unborn child.

What seemed like an eternity was actually only minutes, and, out of breath, I stopped running and panted as a stitch attacked my side. Antoine smiled at me as he stood by a tree and placed his back up against it. He was immaculate. There were no signs of sweat on his brow, while I, quite the opposite, looked a mess. My hair stuck to my chin as I tried to get back some of the breath I had lost in our run.

"We can't hide here all day, you know," Antoine remarked as he took a swig out of a small tin canister.

"Yeah . . . Just give me a minute," I panted.

He looked back in the direction we had come and raised an eyebrow.

"What is it?" I asked.

"I dare say things are going to get pretty messy."

"What do you mean?"

"They're close, Giselle. We cannot outrun them, but if I were to, say, do this." He clasped his hands together, and muttered something under his breath. The ground around us began to shake. From a distance, I could hear the screams and shouts of the men hunting us.

"What was that?" I asked, amused.

"That was a little something I picked up from Bylun. The old man is quite the master of destruction," he laughed.

"Right, so . . . what do we do now? Obviously, we can't stay here. Where do we go?"

He walked over to me and placed his hands on either side of my head. He looked deep into my eyes and I saw a flicker of something I had seen in Leonid. He smiled at me before he kissed me on my nose.

The area around me began to spin. Dizziness interrupted my concentration and left my head reeling from the speed with which we spun. I could barely hear him when he spoke softly, his voice echoed in my mind as I drifted off to a world far from there.

"Now, sweet Princess, you sleep."

J.A. Lynch

Within the Shadows